When Do You Tell The Truth?

ANUPAM BANDYOPADHYAY

Edited By - NAMRATA RAY

notionpress.com

INDIA • SINGAPORE • MALAYSIA

ISBN 979-8-88849-646-6

DEDICATION

This Novel is dedicated to all nature lovers

Contents

CHAPTER 1

THE SUDDEN MEET

It was a coincidence; they met each other after twenty years at a wedding ceremony. Both looked at each other and were speechless for a while. After all, a lot had changed in twenty years, not a short time. It was unexpected for both as he had left Jabalpur for almost twenty years. The situation had confused them; they tactfully ignored each other and busied themselves with their friends. Both had the same feelings. If the incident somehow came to be known here, it would be embarrassing for them both. Even at this age, both were not prepared to accept the truth. The man, fifty years of age and the lady, around forty-five years, stayed in the same city, Jabalpur, for twenty years. The man, was a Lecturer at Jabalpur college and the lady, was a scientist in a research organization, The man was born and brought up in Jabalpur, and they had been staying there for three generations. The lady initially stayed in Jabalpur alone for a few years, and after the superannuation of her father, her parents came there permanently to stay with her. She, the only daughter of her parents, was a brilliant student all along and an upright woman.

The man had joined the dinner after formally wishing the newly married couple. Mr and Mrs Venugopal were busy in the dining hall, looking after their guests. Mrs Shanta Venugopal approached the man, enquiring whether the arrangements were fine. Suddenly, the man noticed that the lady was coming toward him. The lady came near his seat and started talking with Mrs Venugopal. He felt nervous and thought it would be best to focus on eating.

Mrs Venugopal asked the lady about her accommodation in the hotel and learnt that it was good and the staff were cooperative, a matter of three days and not a big deal. Mrs Venugopal was saying to her that she could spend time with them at their home the entire day and only retire to her hotel room for the night. They were recapitulating their school days for a while, and Mrs Venugopal was introducing her to the other guests as her best friend ever since school days. The man had noticed that the lady was sneaking a look at him for a moment and turned her gaze. She had given the company to Mrs Venugopal and involved herself in taking care of the guests' dinner. After dinner, the man met Mr Niranjan Venugopal to formally say goodbye. Mr Venugopal asked about the taste and quality of the food, and the man highly appreciated it. After saying good night to Mr and Mrs Venugopal, the man left.

The lady kept herself busy in conversation with others to avoid the man throughout the evening but noticed that the person had left after giving her a look. She felt relieved after he went and realized that the person was stubborn like before. She had found the man had put on some weight, gained a few grey hairs and a spectacle, though his physique and elegant appearance had not changed. The lady had felt bad and was curious to know about his current status, a women's basic instinct. She thought she would ask her friend before leaving Bangalore.

After the wedding reception was over, Mr Venugopal's driver dropped the lady at her hotel. She didn't notice the man on the opposite side of the road, following her entry. The receptionist informed her that a person was asking about her an hour back, might be an old friend, he had said he would come the next day with a big surprise. She smiled, didn't ask anything about the person and went to her room. She thought to herself that the person was none but the man who met her at the wedding party. But how did he know where she was staying? Suddenly, she realized that Jayanth Viswanathan, whose daughter was her daughter's best friend, was staying at the same city. Only the Venugopal family and her daughter knew about her hotel. Jayanth Viswanathan, a widower, had moved to Bangalore years back. Probably Pritha had told her father about her hotel. If that man wanted to talk with her, he could have done so at the party.

She had freshened up and gone to bed, and a swarm of memories flooded her. She thought that anything could happen in life, she would have never expected to meet this man again in her life after that incident. That day, was the worst day of her life when she was waiting for a whole week, and he didn't show up to meet her parents. She had felt restless and tried to contact his colleagues and even his family for a month but didn't get any information about him. She came to know that he was missing for a week and that the local Police had been informed. Almost every day since then, she had tried to get information about him but had failed. She came to know from his cousin that only his academic certificates, one suitcase and a few garments were missing from his room. The police force had assured them that he had left at his own will and would come back when he felt comfortable, that it was not a kidnapping. She had waited, long and hard, but the man seemed to have disappeared forever. Initially, she was trying to find out the reasons behind it. She had talked with many of his colleagues and a few close friends; none of them could give any clue about his sudden disappearance. Most of them indirectly expressed their views about the misunderstanding between both of them. She didn't try to convince them because it was useless as they were engaged and would marry shortly. Even the Police had suspected and interrogated her during their investigation and ultimately concluded that she had no hand in it, and the case was dismissed after two years. Why he disappeared was a mystery for many years to her. She had never expected to meet him again, but she was shocked and felt sad after seeing him at the wedding ceremony. She was confused and couldn't decide whether she would meet him or just avoid him.

She had spent the worst times of her life in those days. Anxiety and hope of his return had turned her into a psychotic patient. She went to the hospital for a month and gradually became recovered. The Doctor had advised her to join work, involve herself in research, and regularly take her medicine without disruption. After six months, she went to the clinic for a check-up, and the Doctor reduced the dose of her medication. She could feel that she was doing better, continued yearly check-ups for the next five years, and finally was taken off her pills. Her parents and relatives were worried all the time. She was so disgusted with this incident and decided not to marry anybody. She was involved in research work, and the girl gradually had forgotten those dark days of her life. Life is unpredictable for everyone, and anything could happen at any time.

She was trying to recapitulate the last visit with him. They had decided to enjoy the whole day together before their wedding, and it was the birthday of Hardik. They had decided to stop meeting after that, until the wedding. Anumita was very excited and had prepared herself to accept Hardik as a husband even before the wedding. Hardik booked a lodge close to Bhedaghat to relax at the hotel and enjoy the night trip to the Marble Rocks. It was the end of February and a whole moon night. Hardik was mad at travelling and a passionate photographer too. Hardik spent most of the time with Anumita discussing his travelling experiences, and she enjoyed that. Sometimes, Anumita expressed her surprise about him travelling alone and asked him how did he overcome boredom.

Hardik always smiled and didn't answer. Anumita, from the first day, had found Hardik was reserved and less talkative, an introvert. She realized that Hardik had lost his parents in his school days and was brought up under his uncle and aunt's supervision in the same house. They were very strict and always took extra care of him, sometimes it was irritating. Hardik never disobeyed them till finishing his college days. After that, they were reluctant as their son was very dull in his studies but exceptionally talented in maintaining their family business. After joining the College as Lecturer, he started travelling alone in India's different parts. He bought a sophisticated and costly camera for photography and enjoyed his life. Every year he made at least four trips alone.

The only pleasure of his life was travelling. Anumita realised that without travelling and photography, Hardik would not lead a happy life. She never expressed her worries to Hardik and realized that he was a perfect and honest gentleman. Even after marriage, she felt he would continue his travel alone, and she had decided not to inhibit his passion after their marriage. She had always encouraged Hardik to travel and publish a book but never received any response; he just smiled. He was on a trip during the Christmas vacation, to probably Jamnagar for one week. After returning, she found Hardik was very depressed for a few days and didn't even meet her for a week, only talked over the phone. Finally, when they met, she asked about his trip but learnt that the trip was disappointing as only a few snapshots were up to the mark, and all others were ordinary. She was astonished to see his passion for photography and the degree of frustration. She was worried about their future married life for the first time but somehow managed to conceal her feelings. Anumita realized that Hardik probably would never compromise his passion for anything in the future.

Anumita thought of their last togetherness at Bhedaghat, where they spent one night, and she found that Hardik was engaged in shooting the Marble rocks most of the time. She felt odd as Hardik didn't concentrate on her at all, and was rather speechless by observing the beauty of the stones on the full moon.

"What a serene ambience!" Hardik whispered to himself.

"Really darling, it's unbelievable and beyond all words. One of the most memorable days of my life," Anumita replied bringing herself closer to Hardik.

"Let me take a snapshot of yours," Hardik replied and engaged himself in adjusting the camera.

Anumita was happy and trying to pose. Hardik looked at her and said, "no need for any pose, Anu, just look at that rock and feel the beauty."

Still, Anumita remembered that dialogue because of an unusual instruction from Hardik. Even her own choice didn't matter for Hardik when photography was concerned. She contradicted this issue and stood in front of the camera in her pose. Hardik understood the matter and, without saying anything, took her photograph. That was the only picture of Anumita clicked by Hardik as he didn't like to click human images. She kept it for a few years in her drawing room; everyone appreciated it and asked about the photographer. She was tired of lying and found that it was not there one day after coming from her laboratory. She didn't ask her parents anything about it, and after that, she had never seen that picture again.

Anumita could not sleep; every incident with Hardik appeared in her mind. She got up from the bed, went to the toilet, washed her face with water properly, drank some water and went to the balcony. She felt better in the fresh air. The road was almost calm and quiet; occasionally, only a few vehicles reached high speed by generating a hissing sound. Suddenly she noticed a man was standing just opposite the road, probably looking at her. Anumita felt awkward and went back to her room. It was the end of the night; she was trying to sleep but couldn't.

After completing the trip to Bhedaghat, both enjoyed a beautiful dinner and returned to the hotel. Anumita had felt nervous as she had never spent a whole night with a man before. She was surprised to observe Hardik; he was calm and timid, with no excitement or expressions. Anumita had gone to change, and Hardik was busy checking the clicks. Hardik was not very satisfied with his clicks and tried to justify his mistakes. After coming from the washroom, Anumita had observed Hardik note down something in his diary.

"Anything wrong?" Anumita said to Hardik.

"Nothing serious; I was noting the mistakes done by me regarding today's snapshots, my old habits," Hardik replied with a beautiful smile.

Anumita was astonished to see his deep passion for photography. She checked the pages and found the individual analysis of the snapshots, its merits and demerits, and said, "hats off you and your passion !" she had exclaimed.

Hardik started laughing and said, "On every trip, I do this after coming to my room at the night and the next morning going out for the new destination. When you love one thing deeply and involve yourself in that, you can't find any time for boredom." Hardik replied with a smile.

"I must appreciate your passion and am beginning to understand the decision to travel alone Anumita replied with laughter.

Hardik knew very well why Anumita laughed, and he said, "that's why I travel on my own because no one could put up with all these practices."

"Okay, feeling sleepy and good night dear," Anumita said with a seductive smile.

"Good night, darling; I will sleep afterwards when I feel sleepy," Hardik replied casually and involved himself in his work.

Anumita went to bed and was irritated about his peculiar attitude. Anumita thought to herself, would it be wise to marry Hardik? Is he sexually active or does he have any sort of mental blockage? The parents allowed Anumita to stay with him before marriage to know his general behavioural pattern. Her father was very progressive and an ex-army officer. They had spent their lives in different parts of India, and after her graduation, they settled down in their hometown, Kolkata. Initially, she had a problem adjusting to their relatives as they were comparably more conservative but very lively and intimate. Her mother was a lovely simple lady, with an affectionate and modern outlook. She always encouraged Anumita to develop her personality by interacting with people, and not listening to others. The justification should be impartial and devoid of any influences. When they heard from Anumita about their Bhedaghat trip and night stay over there, both supported it. Anumita's mother had told her that it was the last chance to know each other closely, and she appreciated their decision. Their wedding would happen within two months, and next week, after talking with Hardik, they will fix up a date for marriage registration. She encouraged her daughter to minutely follow every matter and justify everything impartially because Anumita would be starting a new life within a brief period. When getting up in the morning, she found Hardik sleeping on the sofa. She realized that Hardik still did not mentally accept her as a wife and had never had sex with any woman before. Otherwise, he, of course, would have utilised this night. She was pleased like every woman, but suddenly a question came to her mind regarding Hardik's sexual health. Hardik, at a glance handsome and masculine, but his face was full of innocence. Anumita didn't disturb Hardik; she had gone for a shower and, when she came back from the washroom, found Hardik reading the newspaper.

"Good morning darling, when did you get up?" Hardik asked.

"Half an hour back, when did you sleep last night? Anumita asked.

An hour after you slept," Hardik replied.

"You get ready; I will order the tea at the reception," Anumita said.

"Okay, give me five minutes," Hardik replied and went to the washroom. They enjoyed tea together, discussing the different plans for their wedding, and Anumita had told her the place of her choice for their Honeymoon. Hardik didn't say anything, just smiled. Both got ready and went for the morning trip to Bhedaghat. Anumita was spellbound after observing the images of rocks in the Narmada, spectacular views. She had noticed that Hardik was busy capturing the images with total concentration. She felt happy after realizing that Hardik was a different human being. His devotion was unparalleled. Anumita had never thought before that to capture the true beauty of Bhedaghat; one should visit it thrice - in the morning, during daytime and the whole moon night. In the early morning, as the number of boats was less in number, one could trek and enjoy the images of rocks in the water of Narmada. During the daytime, reflected sunlight on the marbles varies from place to place; somewhere, it becomes pink, brown and green to black, depending upon the light intensity. On the full moon, spectacular bluish and green rocks were visible. Suddenly, Anumita realized that Hardik was looking at her and smiling.

"Thinking so deeply by seeing the rocks indicates you fell in love with nature," Hardik said with a smile.

"Yes, of course, anyone would fall in love; I am fully lost. I wouldn't forget the beauty of Bhedaghat in my lifetime," Anumita said with enormous satisfaction.

"I observed you; you were immersed in the beauty of nature, you had forgotten my presence," Hardik softly said.

"Yes, absolutely I was, and it should be like that," Anumita replied.

"I liked to lose myself in the natural beauty and don't like to be disturbed at that moment, so I travel alone," Hardik boldly said.

Anumita hadn't heard this voice before in Hardik, a particularly stubborn type of voice. She realized that Hardik never compromised with his passions. A husband or wife couldn't be always delighted with each other. Apart from his madness of travelling and photography, he was a true gentleman and an excellent human being.

"Have you any ideas about how these rocks formed and how they became like this?" Hardik asked.

"As such, no ideas; I will be happy if you tell me the geological basis of these amazing rocks," Anumita said.

"Geological as well as other information I will tell you, sure you will like it. But right now, we will have to check out of the hotel room, and on the way to return, I will tell you everything about this," Hardik said.

They reached the hotel and checked out at the proper time. They had their breakfast in a nearby restaurant and booked a car for Jabalpur. Bhedaghat is 25 km from Jabalpur city and hardly a forty minutes' drive. Anumita's home was in the city, and Hardik had to go another 10 km, he lived in the suburbs. Hardik told her about the Bhedaghat Marble rocks in the car. She still remembered his description as it was the last discussion with Hardik, and several times Police officers had asked about the previous conversations between them. Bhedaghat, the village that found Marble rocks, is about two kilometres long gorge. This long gorge has gleaming white cliffs that transform into stunning pink, brown and black shades as the sunlight makes its way across the sky. Those rocks were formed millions of years back and are made up of Magnesium and Limestone. They were the results of seismic upheavals. The river Narmada cut its way through the stone and formed one of the most spectacular tourist spots, the gorge of Marble rocks. This area was ruled by Mauryan, Gupta and the Gond tribals in different eras. According to Hindu mythology, the black rock is demarcated as the Kal Bhairav, one of the many incarnations of Lord Shiva. After some distance, the river has fallen as Dhauladhar waterfall, and according to the mythology, that point has been considered the gateway to heaven. It believes that Indra, the king of gods, had committed a terrible crime and was sentenced to life on earth as an insect. Eventually, he obtained his release and returned by this way to his abode.

Hardik told her about the Bhedaghat and expressed it in such a fantastic way that Anumita was mesmerized.

Even after twenty years, his last expression reverberated in her ears. Anumita successfully crossed every barrier of life except her wedding. Her parents never created any pressure for getting married to another person. Instead, they always told her marriage shouldn't be the only goal of life, and that everyone should have their own choice in taking decisions and leading life to their liking.

Hardik drove his car and was very unmindful after leaving the wedding party. The reception hall was not very far from his residence. Hardik had reached his home within five minutes, unlocked the door, entered the house, and went straight to the washroom. He splashed water on his face and shoulder and felt better. He had noticed that restlessness and dizziness occurred after any type of excitement for a few years. He had changed and taken out the album. He looked at the only picture of Anumita and observed it. He uttered to himself, yes, the lady he met in the wedding ceremony, was none but Anumita. Hardik immediately looked at another picture, a deep breath came out unknowingly, and Hardik felt; distress and discomfort. He was mesmerized by seeing the similarities between the two pictures though it was almost a regular practice for him. Whenever he thought deeply about Anumita, he compared the two pictures. He was restless and started walking into the room. Even after twenty years, he had never removed Anumita from his mind. Anumita had married, as Hardik came to know from their conversation during dinner time, a few hours back, and had a daughter. He learnt from their discussion that her daughter was in standard nine in a convent in Kochi, and she will be going there after attending this wedding ceremony. Hardik was worried and felt awkward as their sudden meeting might not be good for her family. Hardik did not doubt that leaving her without any intimation shocked her. He always considered himself crude, wrong and a traitor. He had decided, this time he will tell her the reason for his disappearance if she will show minimum interest to know the fact, might be the last meeting with her in this life. Hardik realized that meeting in Bangalore would be risky for both.

Should he ask his friend Venugopal about Anumita? But they would suspect him as he had never asked anything related to any lady before. Hardik had only a few close friends, and Venugopal was one of them. Mrs Venugopal considered him a brother and tried several times for his marriage. Hardik never responded and ignored her with his dubious smile. He had hidden from them the truth of his hometown, had only told them he had lost both of his parents in his school days, and his uncle and aunt brought him up in their village, twenty kilometres away from Jabalpur. He never disclosed his past to anyone, and most of his office colleagues were of the notion that the Geological Survey of India was his first employer. Nobody knew that he had served at a college for three years as a Lecturer of Geology at Jabalpur College.

He tried to sleep as the night was almost over and ultimately fell asleep.

CHAPTER 2

HARDIK – THE TRAVELLER

Hardik had such a soothing personality that everyone liked him. He never hurt anyone, and everyone appreciated his patience and respect for others. His colleagues loved listening to his travel experiences and admired his photography. They showed their reverence for his passion and devotion to work.

After joining the GSI, Hardik was not very comfortable, and his introverted nature indirectly helped him. Most of their colleagues were curious about him as he was handsome and unmarried. Many unmarried female colleagues had shown their interest to make friendships with him, but Hardik very nicely managed it with his polite, endearing person. He loved Venugopal's nature from the first day, a true gentleman in every aspect. He never interfered with the personal matters of anyone but had equal relationships with each colleague. Hardik and Venugopal were intimate with each other as they joined on the same day in the same designation. Gradually, they become officers. Hardik usually avoided meeting personally at their homes, but he took part in different official functions and got introduced.

He realized that most of his colleague's wives were very curious about him and tried to set him up with their relatives. Mrs Shanta Venugopal, an exceptionally good woman, loved him like her brother. Every year Hardik was invited for dinner on their marriage anniversary, the only guest. On the last anniversary, she had scolded him for the trip to Kedarnath alone. Hardik had shown them the pictures he had clicked; both were speechless and appreciated them a lot.

Hardik had mentioned to Niranjan and Shanta a peculiar experience of this trip. Shanta insisted on telling the incident as she loved Hardik's description; it was always accurate and attractive. Hardik also felt good after sharing his travel experiences with this couple; both of them were excellent listeners. He started his speech after a few minutes of silence.

Hardik had started trekking at 4.30 a.m. from Gourikund. It was almost sixteen kilometres walking distance, and he had the plan to stay at Kedarnath for two days. It was pretty dark, but people had started trekking, and a few horse riders were also there. Hardik had noticed that a young boy and two young girls, in a group, were enjoying their trek, 'Har Har Mahadev' sounds had broken the silence of the sleeping mountain. All were enjoying the journey initially, but gradually their speed became less as the road's stiffness increased. The Sun rose around 6 a.m., and the mountains and clouds became visible. He was engaged in clicking some snaps, standing in a corner. Two girls and one boy, whom he had met at the start of the journey just walked past him, chatting.

"I had found they were very comfortable in their trekking, and there was no sign of exhaustion in any of them. Other people were resting in different places and frequently drinking water. We had done almost 4 km of walking, and the path gradually became stiffer and stiffer. After walking another half kilometre, we reached the Jungle, chatted and enjoyed a light breakfast and tea. I found three friends enjoying their breakfast with lots of conversations. They looked at me and smiled gently, and I reciprocated. I saw that all three were full of life and learnt from their discussions that one of the girls would be the boy's wife shortly. The second girl was the close friend of that young boy. They had finished their breakfast and started trekking. I left that place in five minutes. I decided not to stop anywhere until I felt tired. Suddenly, the rain started, and thankfully I was wearing a raincoat. During trekking to the Kedarnath, frequent rain was a common experience for pilgrims; it could rain anytime, and most people wore raincoats except a few, including those three friends. They continued their trekking without wearing raincoats, and I was behind them. The road was very narrow and risky too. Everyone cautiously stepped because it was muddy and slippery. The young boy almost wrapped his would-be wife in his arms and walked very slowly and cautiously, the other girl just behind them. I was hardly five meters apart from that girl.

Suddenly, the girl, who was walking in front of me, slipped and fell on the muddy path, and accidentally she hit the girl in front of her. She lost her balance and fell into the abyss, shrieking in fear. The situation was unbelievable; the boy was speechless, and his close friend was trying to stand up, and just behind her, I was standing like a statue. Suddenly the boy started crying and shouted, seeking help. His howling reverberated in the hills. Everyone from the surroundings gathered within a minute and asked about the fact. All came to know that one lady had slipped and fallen in the deep gorges. All of us were standing still. One of the people asked the girl's name and started to call her by it, in hope that she might have survived the fall.

Then everyone started calling by her name, but there was no response. The second girl had tried to stand up with the help of others and was howling on her own. I was shocked and looked at the girl. Suddenly, she asked me to inform the local rescuers. Many of them tried to notify the registration office and local police station. A few young guys helped the boy and the second girl moved them away from there and provided some water. Both of them were howling, and the girl frequently lost her senses. About fifteen people stopped trekking and accompanied them. I was still speechless and couldn't believe my own eyes, what I had seen a few minutes back. I was the only person who was there during her fall.

After waiting for about thirty minutes, local rescuers finally came and immediately became involved. I spent another fifteen minutes there and left the place, not feeling well. The base camp was Bhimbali, from where Kedarnath would be another 10.5 kilometres. Hardik had tried to forget the incident by concentrating on nature but couldn't. He probably wouldn't in his lifetime. He stopped to see a beautiful waterfall after crossing the Lingcholi, somehow took a picture and started walking.

After reaching Bhimcholi, he washed his face and was feeling a little better. He ordered tea and was trying to come to terms with what he had seen. If he was not wrong, the other girl slipped intentionally to hit the girl's leg so that she, and it had been done with such accuracy that those who were very close to her and observed her only, understood the incident. It was a cold-blooded murder, and he was shocked after watching that incident. The girl somehow realized that he was the only person who had watched the incident, and probably that's why she pretended to lose her senses frequently. "I was trying to remember the incident and felt nauseous. I washed my face with cold water again, had some tea, started trekking and almost trekked non-stop. Around 2 pm, I reached there, booked a hotel and immediately bathed with warm water. I had my lunch and was trying for a nap but couldn't. The only question that repeatedly came to my mind was, why this conspiracy? They were intimate friends; at least, that's what I had felt having watched them for a few hours and hearing their conversations."

"It was simply a preplanner murder and a love triangle issue," Shanta said.

"Did you get any more information about this incident during your return?" Niranjan asked.

"Yes and that was, even more, scaring, though I got the information from a tea seller of a Kedarnath," Hardik replied.

"Please continue, brother," Shanta said with excitement.

Hardik had smiled and resumed. "The following day, I had planned to visit some nearby places but physically didn't feel well. I took a rest until late morning and felt better. After breakfast, I went out to Kal Bhairav temple, which was not very far from Kedarnath temple. The scenic beauty was excellent, and the climate was perfect. The scorching sun and the blowing of cold air created a beautiful feeling. One can see the entire Kedarnath Valley from there, but the fascinating aspect for me was the deep blue sky with the moving milky white clouds. I was standing there for more than half an hour. The place was a few meters before the Kal Bhairav temple. I took several snapshots from there and felt better, a great relief for me. The white clouds were so busy covering the mountain, I had enjoyed their hide-and-seek game and hadn't seen such floccules of white cotton-like clouds in my lifetime. A snow-covered peak was glittering in the sunshine. I was mesmerised and, for the first time, forgot to take any snapshots of that. I returned to Kedarnath and ordered tea in the tea shop. I found some local people discussing yesterday's incident. I was astonished to hear that the girl was rescued with severe injuries as she had fallen and was obstructed by the trees. Rescuers found her in cold condition within three hundred feet and immediately transferred her to the nearest hospital, but the second body did not see them so far. I couldn't resist myself and asked, "second body? Did somebody else fall too?"

One of them replied, "yes, Sir, but the second girl had committed suicide after one hour of the first incident."

After hearing about the incident, I was shocked. I returned to the hotel. In the evening, I went to the temple, sat through the prayer, and felt better. The ambience was peaceful, with pin-drop silence everywhere. I had felt a sense of peace within me. I went back to my hotel and came to know from the hotel manager that within 5 km on the southwest side of the temple, there was a beautiful lake. It served as a water reservoir for supplying water to the entire valley and other adjacent places during summer. Another 3 km downward, was the glacier, the best spot for photography. I had decided to go there the next day after breakfast, and it would hardly take 5 hours to go and return. The manager had told me to follow the trek route. The next day, I started according to the directions and was astonished to visit both places. I had noticed the glamour of nature during that trip and had never seen such types of green, blue and white colours. The lake's water was green; the sky was blue while the glaciers were milky white, a spectacular contrast, and I had captured many snapshots of those places with my mind's eye. I went back to my hotel and had lunch. I couldn't forget the incident, and all this time, one question scrambled in my mind, what was the motive of that girl? She had tried to kill her friend, and when she failed, she committed suicide. I had a realization that it was a triangular love affair. I was the only eyewitness to the attempted murder case. I felt nervous and confused.

In the evening, I went to the temple premises to observe the prayer and found many people watching the prayer ceremony. The wind was chillier than yesterday, and I felt cold. At sharp 6.30 pm, the prayer started, and everyone watched it with complete respect. Suddenly, I saw one young girl coming from behind the temple. The girl couldn't walk correctly and was shabby and dirty. She was searching for someone as her eyes moved continuously. Suddenly her vision fixed on me, and I was scared. I was astonished as no one else noticed that girl as if nobody was there. I was afraid and removed my eyes in the other direction. After a while, I turned my eyes but couldn't see anyone there anymore. Immediately I went back to my hotel and, on the way, frequently looked back whether she was following me or not. But I couldn't find anyone. After reaching my room, I had an early dinner and tucked myself under the quilt to sleep. It was freezing, and I couldn't sleep properly. Again and again, the whole incident crossed my mind. I spent almost a sleepless night and got up early in the morning for my return. On the way to where the incident happened, I crossed carefully and did not find anything. In Lingcholi, I stopped for breakfast and found a few local people talking about the same topic. I overheard them and learnt the same version that I had heard at the tea shop in Kedarnath. Without showing any curiosity, I left the place and, around 1 pm, reached Gourikund."

"Human behaviour is really unpredictable," Niranjan said.

"It was preplanner, and the second girl must have been jealous of their relationship. She may have loved the boy from the early days, but the boy loved her as a true friend, not as a life partner," Shanta said.

"I agree. A dangerous triangular love story. When she found the would-be wife survived, lost her last hope and tried to commit suicide," Hardik said.

"Right, and she had lost her mental balance," Shanta said.

"But what about that girl you had seen during the evening prayer?" Niranjan asked.

"Initially, it was mysterious for me as I don't believe in ghosts. Then I had convinced myself that I must have seen a poor, physically and mentally challenged beggar woman. My mind was disturbed, and all the time I was thinking about that incident and so I had imagined I had seen that girl from the incident, as I was scared," Hardik replied.

Niranjan and Shanta didn't respond regarding this issue as both believed in ghosts. Shanta arranged the dinner, and they enjoyed it together.

He asked himself why all these topics came to his mind today. Hardik realized that after seeing Anumita again, all his worst experiences in real life came rushing back to his mind after almost twenty years. He had seen Anumita in Venugopal's house a few hours back, and it was unexpected. After leaving her at Jabalpur, he initially thought of her every day, and gradually it faded away. During his travel time, he was free from a past life and enjoyed life by travelling and photography, a great reliever of his sadness. He never shared his pain with anyone till now. Many of his colleagues suggested that he should get married as everyone needs the company of some close one in old age. Hardik never expressed his feelings to others, just smiled and kept mum. How could he convince others about his dark part of life? If he told the truth, everyone would have blamed him. He spoiled an innocent young girl's life. No one considered his values, not even Anumita. But after seeing Anumita and knowing that she had a daughter, Hardik felt some relief.

Anumita was a bold, upright and broad-minded lady. Probably, she didn't hide the entire incident from her husband before marriage. He thought several times that if he had told the truth to Anumita, how would she have reacted? Anumita probably would have accepted him, but Hardik wouldn't. He always felt ashamed when remembering those things. The inhibition of Hardik taking Anumita as a wife was the main barrier between them. If Hardik would hide the fact from Anumita and in future when she could come to know the facts, she definitely would be hurt and hate his entire family.

The situation would be so complicated that he could not tell the truth behind this; both lives would be finished. These reasons forced him to end the relationship and go far away from Anumita. Hardik still remembered when he had come to know everything from his uncle and decided to leave this place without informing anyone. He had arranged everything within two days, his academic credentials, documents from the Bank, hard cash, accessories for photography and some valuable garments. He packed up carefully so that no one suspected him, and finally, when everyone slept off in the night, he eventually left the house with immense sadness. After reaching the railway station, he bought a Bangalore ticket and waited for the train. It was a cold foggy night, and only a few passengers were present. Hardik had wrapped himself with warm garments in such a way that no one could identify him easily. After waiting half of the night, he boarded and reached Bangalore. It was ultimately a new city for him, and after struggling for almost two months, he got this job. He was so upset that he usually avoided people and had no interest in travelling or photography. He had spent all the time in office work and realized that he had moved past the depression slowly with each passing day. After leaving home, the first year was horrible for him; only he knew how he had spent those days. He never disclosed anything to anyone, and his life was like living hell. He had lost all his hope and lived like a robot, shuttling between office and home, nothing else.

The only person in his office who always tried to cheer him up was Niranjan Venugopal. Every day he spent some time during lunch break and at the end of the duty hours. Initially, his colleagues thought he was too proud, and Niranjan probably had too, but they ultimately started to love him as the days went by. Niranjan had perhaps realized that he was going through

rough times and never asked him anything but always stayed with him as a companion. Niranjan, a kind-hearted person, intelligently inspired him with a positive attitude. After knowing his passion for travelling and photography, he arranged a trip to Madikeri for three days. Niranjan, Shanta, their only daughter Shreya and Hardik. That was the first time Hardik had touched his camera after leaving Jabalpur. The trip was a fantastic one. Niranjan drove his car, and it was one of his best road journeys. The natural beauty from Mysore to Madikeri was unforgettable. Initially, he was inactive and hardly spoke, but Shanta and Shreya gradually involved him in their conversations. They had all together enjoyed a lot in different spots of Madikeri, especially the sunset at Raja's seat. Hardik had taken a few snapshots of the natural beauty and them. Niranjan had the plan to return to Bangalore via another route, but he changed his decision and encouraged him to take photographs when he heard that Hardik loved photography. He felt better after this trip and realized that only his passion could help him to live better. He started, and as time passed, the wound gradually healed.

CHAPTER 3

THE RECEPTION PARTY

When Anumita woke up, it was fifteen minutes to 10 am. She was embarrassed as she was supposed to reach Shanta's house within 10 am. She had called Shanta and told her that she will be getting there within 10.30 am. She had come to know the car would be there. Accordingly, she felt there was no need to be worried as everything was running late at their home. Anumita made her tea and went to the balcony; the road was full of traffic, and the orchestra of noise irritated her. Suddenly, she realized a man was watching her from the opposite side of the road. She had finished her tea and came back to her room. She was scared and had decided to inform the reception when she would be out for Shanta's house. She had gone to the washroom and had got dressed quickly. Suddenly, she thought, if Hardik was there, what she would do. Would she talk with him? What if he didn't recognize her? She felt embarrassed and decided to deny him. He was the man who had broken her dreams. Due to him, she had given her parents a serious cause of worry and had put them in an awkward situation in front of relatives and friends, though they never said a single word to her.

Anumita went to the reception and informed them about that man. She came to know that the man, every night and morning stood over there without disturbing anyone, probably a mentally challenged person. They assured Anumita not to worry. If that person misbehaved with her, they would take necessary actions. Anumita had told them he never did so, neither gestured anything to her, only gave her a vacant look. She left reception and got in the car. The driver had started after wishing her good morning. the evening before, she had hardly taken note of the route as she met her friend after a long time. Moreover, she was also worried about the meeting with Hardik. She tried to divert her mind by looking outside. Bangalore city, the most popular cosmopolitan one in India, grew a lot due to its climate, cleanliness and greenery. The high risers covered the two sides of the road with plenty of trees. The pavements were clean, which reflected the civic sense of the general people. She had reached her destination within fifteen minutes, and on the way, she found yesterday's marriage hall.

After reaching there, her friend requested her to have some breakfast. Anumita was feeling hungry and had complied. Anumita had realized that she was a bit unmindful and tense too. Her eyes were searching for someone. She couldn't ask anyone about him but expected him in her imagination very much; she was feeling a peculiar discomfort within herself. Probably Shanta had noticed that and asked, "any problem? not looking fresh, darling."

"Nothing much; it might be due to sleeplessness last night," Anumita replied with a pale smile.

"Yes, you need to rest. Come with me," Shanta said.

"Where? I will be with you like school days," Anumita said.

"In my room, you need some rest, and before lunch, I will call you," Shanta said with full command.

"Still, you keep your room just like the school days, like school prefect?" Anumita replied with laughter.

"I wouldn't like to miss you at the evening party; take a rest so that by that time, you will be looking fresh, my sweetheart," Shanta said.

Shanta almost forcefully took her into the room, arranged everything properly so that she could sleep without any disturbance, closed the door and left. Anumita was not feeling well, which might have been due to her anxiety and depression. All memories were disturbing her like last night, but she tried to overcome them by thinking about her daughter. Tomorrow she would buy a few garments for her daughter from nearby shopping malls, and the day after tomorrow, she would be on the morning flight to Kochi. She would have only one day in her hand and should be careful about her health. She had decided to bring her daughter with her to the hotel if the principal sister allowed and arrange a trip to Munnar as her daughter requested. After six months, she would be meeting her this time. Anumita fell asleep.

"Anu, get up; someone would like to meet you," Shanta said.

"Oh, when I slept off?" Anumita replied after waking up and watching the time.

"Oh, 4 pm! Why didn't you wake me up? Who wanted to meet me?" Anumita asked so many questions to Shanta, at a time.

Shanta started to laugh and said, "one by one, darling. I came here twice to call you, but you were in a deep sleep. You needed rest, and so I had my lunch without you. I realized that you need rest and sleep more than food. Your boyfriend wanted to meet you and was waiting for you in the guest room, go and meet him. After that, get ready for the party, and if you feel hungry, have some food."

"Boyfriend?" Anumita asked.

"The man said he was your friend and would like to meet you urgently," Shanta said, pinching her.

"My friend in Bangalore? Except for you, I have no one in Bangalore, strange! You know very well that I had a limited number of friends, and all of them were female, " Anumita replied and went to meet him after quickly freshening up.

Anumita was a bit nervous and scared by thinking of Hardik. If the person was Hardik, what would she do? She had decided not to discuss anything here and would just maintain the formalities. She entered the room and found Mr Viswanathan was waiting. After seeing her, he got up from the sofa and they wished for each other. Both met several times in Cochin on different occasions at their daughter's school.

"Sorry to disturb you at the wedding party," Viswanathan said.

"It's alright, but how did you get this address?" Anumita asked.

"I went to your hotel, and they told me about it," Viswanathan said.

"How did they know my friend's residence?"

"Who booked your hotel?" Viswanathan asked.

"Oh! I understood, actually, after seeing you here I was surprised. Anyway, the day after tomorrow, I will be going to Cochin. If you would like to send something to your daughter, you can give it to me," Anumita humbly said.

"I will drop you a small packet tomorrow evening. If you wouldn't be present in the hotel, I will keep it at the reception," Viswanathan said.

"Okay, but you could have just informed me by phone, unnecessarily you wasted your time and had trouble reaching here," Anumita replied with a gentle smile.

"My daughter had instructed me to meet you physically, not by a formal telephonic call and to check if you needed anything or wanted to visit any place as tomorrow is Sunday," Viswanathan humbly said.

"Yes, that will be great, tomorrow I will be ready within 11 am, and if possible, you can pick me up from my hotel and we will enjoy the city," Anumita said with joy.

"That will be fantastic, and my daughter will be so happy to know this" Viswanathan replied.

"No need to disclose it right now; tomorrow during lunch, we will call both of them," Anumita said, laughing.

"Okay, it will be a great surprise for both and both of them would be very happy," Viswanathan said.

Shanta had entered the room with a maid, and she instructed her to keep the food and coffee on the centre table. Anumita had introduced Viswanathan to Shanta, and she briefed both of them about each other. Anumita had told her about their plan for tomorrow.

"Okay, but remember one thing, dinner should be with me in my house," Shanta said.

"Okay, my lord," Anumita replied with a smile.

"You both finish your coffee and excuse me as I have to arrange many things for the evening," Shanta said and went out.

Both talked a bit and finished their coffee; Anumita went with Viswanathan up to his car to see him off. Anumita had told Shanta to ask the driver to drop her at the hotel after coming back. Shanta replied to her that the driver was waiting in the car, and she instructed her to come back by seven pm, and the driver will be waiting at the hotel. Anumita noticed that it was already five pm and rushed to the car. Shanta was the only person to whom Anumita never felt any hesitation to say anything. She loved Anumita like her own sister, and still, a beautiful understanding existed between the two. Anumita was present in Shanta's marriage about twenty years back. Shanta had an early marriage, and after that, she did her master's degree. Anumita had never seen such a balanced lady in her lifetime. Both shared everything over the phone initially, but gradually, she restricted herself after the tragic incident in her life. She had hidden the facts from her. Shanta was worried about her marriage, but she told her not to marry anyone just for the sake of it. When she adopted a girl child, Shanta was so happy and said that she felt proud of Anumita. She didn't discuss anything with Shanta about her love affair with Hardik. She had thought that, after the wedding date was set, she, would surprise her, but the date never was fixed. She was so depressed and hid the shame of her life from everyone. Except few of her close relatives and some local people, no one knew about their relationship, and it was only a seven-month affair between Anumita and Hardik.

"Madam, your hotel," the driver said.

"Oh," she replied and realized, she had been unmindful, immersed in all these thoughts.

"Madam, I would be in the parking zone, and when you are ready to go, you just give me a call," the Driver said.

"Okay," Anumita replied and went to reception for the key.

"Madam, one gentleman had come to meet you, and we provided the home address of Mr Venugopal as he had told us it was urgent," the receptionist said.

"Yes, he went there and met me; thank you for your concern," Anumita replied with a smile and went to her room.

She had freshened up and engaged herself in doing make-up. Anumita always preferred simple make-up, she got ready and noticed it was only a few minutes to six pm. Suddenly, she received a phone call, and it was from her daughter. Anumita had felt her daughter was very excited because, after almost six months, both would see each other the day after tomorrow. She asked for every detail of her make-up for the marriage party. She wondered whether her friend's father contacted her or not. Anumita told her that Mr Viswanathan had met her and they talked a lot. She had told her she would call her the next day, as she was getting late for the party. Anumita disconnected the line, locked the door and went near the car parking zone. She called the driver and was waiting for the car. Suddenly she found that the same man was standing on the opposite side of the road and looking at the hotel's balcony. Anumita was curious, crossed the street, and stood beside him without saying a word. The man ignored her and was looking at the terrace quietly. Anumita had noticed that the person was neat and clean, well-suited and not less than sixtyfive years old. She had found people crossing him, and a few of them looked at him and tried to find out what the man was looking at, but that person didn't bother to answer. Without asking anything further, she crossed the road and found the driver was waiting for her.

Anumita had reached Shanta's house; Shanta came near her, set a Jasmine garland on her hair, and complimented her saree. Shanta realized that everyone had reached out except her brother, not her real brother. Anumita had noticed carefully that Hardik was not there, and she had a peculiar type of feeling, neither happy nor sad.

"Shanta, make a call to your brother and ask him about his current status," Niranjan said.

Shanta immediately called him and came to know that he had just come from the office and was extremely tired; if he felt good, he would go to the party directly. So, as not to waste time unnecessarily for him. Shanta had told her husband everything, and all of them went towards the bus. Anumita felt comfortable as Hardik was not present. It was only half an hour's drive to the party hall. They warmly received them, and all were happy after their arrival; the bride and groom were busy with the invitees. Shreya, daughter of Venugopal, was excited to see her relatives and told her husband about them. Both had come to receive them, and Shanta hugged her daughter.

"Looking pretty, my child," Shanta affectionately said.

Shreya was looking so pretty and fresh. Both of them talked with Anumita and asked about her next plan. Anumita told them about her next destination and invited them for a few days to Jabalpur. Both assured her to visit her place whenever they got a fair chance.

"Daddy, what about Hardik uncle? He promised to be present and take some pictures of mine," Shreya replied with disappointment.

"He must have a problem. Otherwise, your uncle would never go back on his commitment," Niranjan replied.

Anumita listened to everything with a sigh of despair. Who knew better than her about Hardik's commitment? Anumita realised that Hardik avoided her and did not have enough courage to accept the truth. He had his passion still, and probably he was enjoying his life in his way. Anumita was angry at his selfishness, expecting him to tell her the truth, not leave her in this way. From their conversations, Anumita had understood that Hardik was probably single as he was present alone at yesterday's party, and Shreya asked only about his uncle, he could be married and divorced as well. No woman would have considered his selfishness and allowed him to fulfil his passion.

"Again, you look depressed and fatigued; what happened to you," Shanta asked.

"Oh, nothing, don't bother about me at least here, enjoy the party and involve yourself with everyone," Anumita r whispered to her.

"Okay, but don't hide any discomfort to me and mind it; I could read your face like school days, seat over there," Shanta ordered her.

"Oh my God! This lady is still like a dictator to me, just like in school days," Anumita replied, laughing.

Anumita was seated on a sofa and was watching others. Suddenly, she noticed that Hardik was entering the hall. Immediately, Anumita turned her head. Hardik had found Niranjan talking with someone, went there and touched his shoulder. Niranjan was so happy to see him and, after saying sorry to the person who had excused him, took Hardik to the main stage.

"Shreya, look here," Niranjan said.

Shreya jumped from her seat, hugged her uncle, and asked, "why so late? I was worried about you."

"I came late from the office and felt tired. I took some rest for half an hour and started. Let me shoot your pictures first," Hardik said.

Hardik was engaged with his camera, Shreya with her husband, and others were waiting for the snapshots. Shanta went to bring her friend, Anumita was talking with someone. She took her photos; Anumita hesitated but couldn't escape from her friend. Shanta told Anumita that Hardik, their family friend, was a fantastic amateur photographer and a lovely gentleman. Anumita was keeping mum and looked at her. Shreya was busy shooting along with her husband, and according to Shreya's choices, Hardik was alive with clicking. She had demanded to take pictures according to her preferred poses, and Hardik, without any instruction, clicked her pictures. Anumita had remembered their last trip, and Hardik's last clicked pictures of her. The best photo of her disappeared like Hardik. She had lost Hardik and herself. Today's Anumita had killed her love, desires and dreams for the future. Most of her emotions were gone forever; she never felt attracted to any male or sexual urges. That's why she had decided not to marry. She only fulfilled her one dream and adopted a girl child. After adopting Anushka at the age of six months, Anumita gradually involved herself with Anushka; day by day, she overcame the shock Hardik had imposed on her.

"Anu, meet my brother, Hardik, a passionate photographer and our family friend too. Brother, Anumita, my best friend ever," Shanta said with excitement.

Both were embarrassed, but Anumita quickly managed the situation and just smiled without saying anything. Hardik reciprocated the same and left where Niranjan was talking with the groom's father. Niranjan introduced Hardik as his colleague and family friend. Hardik felt awkward and somehow had told him hello. Anumita had realized that Shanta didn't suspect anything as she was busy with the others. Otherwise, she would have asked her about the unusual behaviour. Mr and Mrs Nair, the in-laws of Shreya, requested everyone to join in the dinner. All of them went to the dining hall and started their dinner.

"Anu, any problem? Again you are looking pale," Shanta whispered.

"Again, you have started; just shut your mouth and take care of others," Anumita whispered.

"Darling, it's not so easy to hide anything from me," Shanta replied with a typical smile.

Anumita was scared and became more nervous. She turned her face and found Hardik was looking at her. She immediately went towards the food court to bring some pickles as she was feeling nauseous. After coming back from the food court, she sat on the sofa and tried to combat the uneasiness. Shanta immediately came to her and asked about her discomfort. Anumita had told her not to worry, it was her everyday problem, and she had gastric issues for two years. Shanta told her not to eat anymore and gave her medicine. Anumita didn't stop her and had observed Hardik watching her. Shanta gave her a tablet and requested Hardik to bring a glass of water. Anumita was upset and felt more discomfort. Hardik brought a glass of lukewarm water and gave it to Shanta.

"Take it immediately; you would get relief within five minutes," Shanta said.

Anumita had taken the medicine and said, "Don't panic, enjoy the moment with everyone, I will be alright within a few minutes,"

"Just keep quiet, and no need to instruct me. How could you travel to Cochin alone after two days? I don't know, and I'm apprehensive about you, " Shanta replied with anxiety.

"Don't behave like this, Shanta; it's simple acidity, and you, still over-conscious about me like School days," Anumita harshly replied.

"Listen, Anu, if this will persist until tomorrow, I will postpone your journey to Cochin," Shanta said and went to the food court.

"Oh, this lady will never change," Anumita said, laughing.

Hardik had heard the conversations and felt that the gastric irritation was due to extreme emotional situations, and he was responsible for that. Hardik departed the place and went to the food court. Anumita was sitting at the same place and gradually getting comfortable. She was embarrassed by her situation and realized that her gastric problems had relapsed after a long time. She knew that hiding something from Shanta was difficult but how could she talk about the darkest part of her life as she had hidden that fact for twenty years before? Anumita had decided never to disclose it to Shanta. Otherwise, she would be disheartened. She will be busy tomorrow with Mr Viswanathan, and the next day early in the morning, she will leave Bangalore. Somehow, she would avoid Hardik, the main root of the problem.

Hardik left the place after saying to his friend Niranjan that he should reach the studio quickly to save the clicked snaps as the camera had opened by mistake. Hardik drove his car and got to his house. He was not feeling well; he felt better after splashing some water on his face and shoulder. He determined this time he would tell everything to Anumita and probably would be the last chance to meet her. For him, Anumita was suffering for twenty years. Hardik was sanguine that she had hidden everything from Venugopal's family. It shouldn't be wise to meet and discuss with her in Bangalore, risky for both. He should be careful. Otherwise, she would suspect that he was indifferent and less curious about anyone, especially women. Hardik was trying to find out how to get information about Anumita, and suddenly he realized that was the correct time to ask about her. He made a call to Shanta.

"Sister, sorry to disturb you as it is already half-past ten. Without informing you, I went out due to an emergency. Moreover, you were busy with your friends and relatives, please don't mind," Hardik said.

"Oh, not at all and your friend informed me. I was worried about my friend, Anumita," Shanta replied.

"Yes, I had noticed that; how is she?" Hardik asked.

"Within half an hour, she became fit and fine. I gave her medicine and was worried about her journey," Shanta replied.

"Journey?" Hardik asked intentionally to know about her detailed programme.

"She came from Jabalpur, and the day after tomorrow morning, she will go to Cochin to meet her only daughter," Shanta replied.

"Sorry, I couldn't get you, Jabalpur, Bangalore, Cochin, and only daughter, complicated issues for me," Hardik replied with a smile.

"She came here to attend the marriage, and on the way, she will meet her only daughter who studies in St. Joseph's Convent in Cochin. I will be worrying for her during her travelling," Shanta replied.

"Simple acidity might be due to disturbances in regular patterns and excitement, don't worry. Anyway, now you need rest. Good night to both of you," Hardik said and cut the connection.

Hardik was happy as he had got his required information. He went to bed and slept off within a few minutes.

Chapter 4

THE FRAGRANCE OF LIFE

Anumita had taken a shower and was feeling better after reaching the hotel. She had talked with Shanta and informed her; that she felt fresh and delicate. Within a few minutes, she would be sleeping, and after getting up in the morning, would give her a call her. Shanta warned her not to hide anything if she felt any discomfort like before and reminded her to take medicine. Anumita assured her, bid her good night and hung up. She went to the balcony to get some fresh air, and found the same person standing in the same place, looking in the same direction as yesterday. Anumita had felt some pathos for that man, thinking about his restlessness and patience. From evening tonight, he stood over there and looked at their balcony. Even in the daytime, he had been standing there for a few hours. What did he watch and why? Was he looking for someone? Anumita hadn't noticed any threatening gesture from that person for a single moment, just a constant vacant look. She went back to her bed, feeling sad. She knew that only people could sympathise with mentally challenged people, not much more to do. Anumita had been trying to remove these thoughts and focus on planning for tomorrow.

She had planned to buy a few things for her daughter and her friend. Her father, Mr Viswanathan, would come tomorrow to pick Anumita up, and within seven pm, he will drop her at Shanta's house. She would also need to arrange her luggage before leaving the hotel with Mr Viswanathan.

The sound of the phone awakened Anumita. It was Shanta, and she was asking about her health. Anumita realized she was late but felt fresh and better. She had mentioned it to her friend and discussed everything about her plan for that day. Shanta had told her to avoid spicy food and take care of herself and stay in touch with her in between, if possible. Anumita assured her and told her not to be worried as she would be with Mr Viswanathan. She made her tea and went to the balcony. The traffic was not as bad as around eight am, and that man was not there. Anumita felt sad thinking about that man again. Many things had come to her mind. Suddenly, she realized it was already late, and much work was left before leaving the hotel. Anumita rushed to the washroom to get ready.

After packing her luggage, she ordered some light breakfast and waited for it. Anumita realized that somehow, she felt some peculiar type of curiosity and inquisition about that person. She had opened the balcony door and searched whether the person was there or not, but she didn't find him. Anumita was trying to remember his profile as she watched him closely the evening before. His face was full of beard and two beautiful red lips below a nice moustache. The person was not dirty and had sharp eyes and a sharp nose like Greek people. The person was handsome and lean, in appearance. Anumita heard the sound of the doorbell and opened the door. A lady was standing with her ordered breakfast. She advised her to keep the food on the table and gave her some tips. The lady was pleased and went out of the room. Anumita finished her breakfast and was waiting for the call from Mr Viswanathan.

After getting the call from Mr Viswanathan, she came down to the reception and found the car was ready to move. They wished each other and Anumita sat beside Mr Viswanathan in the front seat. Before starting the car, he asked Anumita about her first destination. Anumita had told him about her marketing plan. Mr Viswanathan drove towards one of the biggest shopping centres in Bangalore. Both engaged in casual talk, and Anumita learned that Viswanathan would be going to Cochin after two months. Anumita had told him she would be going there after her daughter's annual examination to bring her daughter home for one month. Anumita had realised that Viswanathan was indifferent and did not respond to this.

"If you don't mind, shall I ask one question?" Anumita said.

"Yes, of course," Viswanathan replied.

"Had your daughter demanded to stay with you instead of the hostel?" Anumita asked.

"Initially, she asked frequently, but gradually she adapted herself, and after becoming friends with your daughter, she never asked further," Viswanathan replied.

"Strange! Same here. But I have decided after completion of her board examinations, I will take her to Jabalpur with me," Anumita said.

"Oh, why not let her stay for two more years?" Viswanathan asked.

"I miss her a lot and realized she did too, but she never expressed it to me, "Anumita replied.

"Daughters were always more comfortable with mothers but my daughter is unfortunate in that aspect," Viswanathan said.

"Yes, that's true, but some fathers, really exceptional like you," Anumita stated.

Viswanathan had stopped the car, and Anumita had found one magnificent shopping mall. Viswanathan had parked the car, and both entered. Anumita found shops of almost all big brands and food courts. Both of them were window shopping, and Viswanathan found Anumita was very excited like every woman.

Viswanathan was laughing on his own and remembered those days that he had spent with his wife. Sujata was crazy about shopping. She was a pretty woman and had something special on her face which attracted everyone, from 18 to 80 years. She called her husband Visu and loved him dearly. They used to work together in the same company.

"Mr Viswanathan, would you like to enter with me in this shop?" Anumita asked.

Viswanathan had noticed it was a ladies' garments shop, and her daughter warned her not to send anything this time as she hadn't any space to accommodate further.

"You go and take your time; I will be sitting outside," Viswanathan replied with a smile.

"Okay," Anumita said and entered the shop.

Viswanathan sat on a bench outside the shop and started thinking about Sujata. After four years of enjoyment of married life, they had a girl child, Pritha. Sujata had resigned from her job and devoted herself to her daughter. Viswanathan had a realization that she was gradually becoming distant from her husband. Sometimes, Viswanathan was irritated by her negligence and was astonished that within four years, she had changed, and her whole world was her daughter as if he didn't exist. Viswanathan didn't tell Sujata anything and had started neglecting her as well. Initially, Sujata hadn't reacted, but after a few months, she started asking about his late coming from the office and avoiding his responsibilities towards their daughter. Thus, the husband-wife family war had started.

"Sorry for the delay," Anumita said with a smile.

Viswanathan turned and said, "It's alright, I was quite comfortable here."

"Mr Viswanathan, I would like to tell you that, lunch will be my treat and it would be according to your choice of cuisine," Anumita boldly said.

"How would that be possible? It's like you came to my home and a treat to me," Viswanathan replied with laughter.

gave me "Nothing is impossible in this Universe, don't force me to skip my lunch," Anumita replied.

"Okay, as you wish, but it would not be wise," Viswanathan replied with dissatisfaction.

After completing her marketing Anumita and Viswanathan went to the food courts and sat comfortably.

"So, I have to choose the menu?" Viswanathan asked.

"Yes, of course," Anumita confidently replied.

"Would you like any drinks?" Viswanathan asked with hesitation.

Anumita realized that if she denied the drinks, Viswanathan wouldn't be able to enjoy the time, so she decided to have some beer. Viswanathan decided to have the same though he had no practice of drinking except occasionally.

"Yes, a bottle of chilled beer," Anumita replied.

"That's good; any specific choice?" Viswanathan asked.

"Not really, but it should be of good quality and a costly one," Anumita replied.

"Okay, let's start with the drinks and will order the main course during our drinks," Viswanathan said and placed the order.

Anumita suddenly remembered that she had forgotten to call Shanta. She immediately called and informed her she was fit and fine now. Shanta wanted to know about her lunch, and Anumita told her to wait in the restaurant. She told Shanta not to worry; she would be getting to her house within 6 pm and ended the call.

"My friend Mrs Shanta Venugopal is a very caring and wonderful human being," Anumita said with a smile.

"I understand, and you came here to attend her daughter's wedding," Viswanathan replied with a smile.

They had started enjoying the beer. Initially, both didn't like it, but gradually both felt fine.

"Your one decision made me uncomfortable," Viswanathan said by sipping his beer.

"Oh! Really? I am so sorry; which decision?" Anumita asked.

"As you said, after the board exam, you would be taking your daughter with you, and how my daughter would react to that, I am doubtful," Viswanathan said.

"That's true; both love each other like sisters and share everything. Shanta and I were like that, and both had faced tremendous pain when we were separated from each other and had to face reality," Anumita replied.

Viswanathan had realized that the situation would be difficult, and both were here to enjoy the day. He changed the topic and asked her how she felt after consuming half a beer bottle.

"I feel nice and relaxed as I am not a frequent drinker," Anumita replied with a pleasant smile.

"Same here; I enjoy it a lot. I only drink during office parties at the request of my friends," Viswanathan replied.

"Every gentleman claim that and when someone asks them how many parties they attended in a month, the gentlemen reply not more than thirty," Anumita replied with laughter.

Viswanathan started laughing and said, "Believe me, people never considered me a gentleman."

Anumita started laughing and reminded him to order the food. Viswanathan ordered their food and realised that he was having an excellent time with a lady after a long time. Anumita had finished her last sip and realised that Viswanathan was looking very bright and happy. Anumita asked Viswanathan casually if she would take his daughter for a three-day short trip to Munnar, and if would he allow it. Viswanathan had understood that it was a preplanner thought, and he told her, he would send the email to Anumita and the Principal Sister.

Viswanathan said, "I can do anything for my daughter's pleasure."

"Thank you so much, Mr Viswanathan; both would be very happy after knowing it," Anumita replied with joy.

"A nice pre-planned programme, but why did all of you exclude me from this excellent plan, I couldn't understand?" Viswanathan said with laughter.

"Pre-planned? With them? I didn't discuss anything about it and kept it a secret to surprise them. Yes, that's my fault for excluding you as I thought you would be busy and might be unable to manage your schedules," Anumita replied.

"Just joking, you were right, being a senior manager of the office, it's very tough to manage leaves, almost at all the times I have to overstay at the office," Viswanathan smilingly said.

"Sorry, I should have included you. It didn't occur to me," Anumita apologised.

"Oh! forget about it; I have one close connection in Hotel Paradise at Munnar; I will book it online there for three days; let me know your specific dates of stay," Viswanathan said and opened his cell phone.

Anumita had given the specific dates, and Viswanathan booked it. Viswanathan forwarded all the documents; told her it was far from the main town but famous for its location.

They had their lunch, and it was around three pm. Anumita had paid the bills, and Viswanathan asked about her next plan. Anumita told him if time permits, she would like to visit Tipu Sultan's Palace for a while, and Viswanathan informed her that it was not far from there, only a few minute's drives.

Viswanathan had started the car and asked her opinion of the shopping mall and the branded stores. Anumita expressed her satisfaction and mentioned that she hadn't seen such a big shopping mall in Jabalpur and many metro cities in India. She liked the behaviour of the shopkeepers, and according to her, the most beautiful part of the shopping mall was its cleanliness.

"Madam, we have reached Tipu Sultan's palace. If you don't mind, I will be in the car, and you, please visit the palace and come back here," Viswanathan said.

"Sure, I will make it around and come back within fifteen minutes," Anumita replied and went to the palace.

Anumita was amazed by seeing the Indo-Islamic architecture-based Palace. The entire Palace had been constructed with teak wood and frescoes. The wooden pillars and balconies were the other beautiful attractions of this Palace. It was the summer palace of Tipu Sultan. The wooden posts were painted with different colours and were still so bright; she loved it.

Anumita went back to the entry gate and found Viswanathan standing outside the car and talking over the phone. After seeing her, Viswanathan raised his hand with a gentle smile. Anumita had crossed the road carefully and stood beside him. Both were seated in the car, and Viswanathan started driving.

"How was the Palace?" Viswanathan asked.

"I loved it, a small one but majestically gorgeous," Anumita replied with great satisfaction.

"That's true, anyway, any other place you would like to visit?" Viswanathan asked.

Anumita watched the time and found it was half past four; she said, "No, straightway to my friend's house."

"Don't worry, I will drop you at your friend's house within forty-five minutes; if you like, we will have a cup of coffee on the way," Viswanathan said.

"That will be fantastic, and around 5 pm, we will have coffee, and this time you will pay," Anumita said with laughter.

Viswanathan started laughing and said, "sorry, I haven't any cash."

"No need for cash; you will pay through a card," Anumita replied with a smile.

"Okay, as you wish," Viswanathan replied with laughter.

Viswanath had realised that almost after a decade, he spent a lovely day with a lady. Anumita, a wonderful human being, has a pleasant personality. But one thing was not clear to him whether she was divorced or widowed. If she was widowed, why didn't she marry again? Even at this age, she had an elegant appearance and attractive looks. Suddenly, he realised that it shouldn't be on his mind, Anumita's private matter. Viswanathan looked at her and found she was dosing off. He had decided to stop the car at the nearest coffee parlour. After driving for another five minutes, he parked the car near a coffee shop, looked at Anumita and found she had woken up.

"Right time for coffee, thank you," Anumita said with excitement.

Both of them entered the shop and were seated in the chairs. Anumita, at a glance, looked at other customers and had found a few seniors were looking at them, young people were busy with their discussions, and only a few ladies were enjoying their coffee either with their boyfriends or husbands. Two ladies were sitting in a chair and talking, frequently looking at them. Anumita felt uneasy and turned her head.

"Do you need anything with coffee? I meant any confectionaries," Viswanathan asked.

"Only coffee, nothing else; if you need any confectionaries, please don't hesitate," Anumita replied.

Both had finished the coffee, felt fresh and had started to return.

Viswanathan dropped her off after discussing her travel details in Munnar and told her to call him if they faced any problems there. Anumita assured him and said sorry again for not including him on the trip.

Shanta was happy to see her friend one hour before the stipulated time. She asked about her health and was glad to know that Anumita hadn't felt any discomfort throughout the day. Anumita went to the washroom, and Shanta went to the kitchen for tea. She knew her from school days and that she loved tea, especially returning from outside.

Anumita, Shanta and Niranjan enjoyed the tea. Anumita gifted a Saree to Shanta and a shirt to Niranjan. Both had liked their gifts, and Shanta asked about her whole day's experiences. Both were glad to know that Anumita loved the city, especially the Tipu Sultan's Palace.

At eight pm, Shanta served dinner, and all the preparations were simple and tasty. Anumita enjoyed the food and had a good time with them. Both dropped her off after dinner at the hotel, and Niranjan assured her that the next day, sharp at seven am, both would pick her up for Airport. Shanta had told her to sleep early and would call her at five am.

CHAPTER 5

THE DISGUISE

The plane landed at Cochin Airport at the scheduled time. Most of the passengers were waiting in their seats as it was a connecting flight to Trivandrum. Anumita had noticed that a maximum of fifteen to sixteen passengers were waiting to deboard. Cochin Airport was around twenty-five kilometres from the city, and the car had charged six hundred last time. Anumita was looking for one who could share the car with her. She had found one lady who was probably alone. After collecting the luggage, Anumita gave the proposal to that lady, and she agreed to share the ride.

Both hired a car and had started their journey. Anumita introduced herself and told her destination. The lady was from Bangalore, and she was going to her brother's house for a wedding. Anumita realized after talking with the lady that she frequently visited Cochin and had known this city from her childhood. She had completed her studies in the same convent where Anumita's daughter studied. She told Anumita about her school days, and she appreciated her wise decision regarding her daughter's education. Anumita realized that she was none but Ranjini Iyer, who received the Bhatnagar Award two years back in Pharmaceutical Chemistry and worked in the Indian Institute of Science as a Senior Scientist for fifteen years. Ranjini was astonished to find out that both were from the same stream, and Anumita was just two years senior. Both had exchanged their professional cards. None of them noticed that a car was following them from the Airport.

The driver dropped her at the said hotel, and Ranjini had gone in the same car. Anumita entered the hotel, dropped her luggage in her room, and freshened herself up. Anumita knew most of the staff as she was an old hotel customer. The manager had arranged their hotel car for her daughter's school. Anumita had started after around thirty minutes of rest to pick up both of them from school. The school would remain closed for four days and including Sunday, it was a total of five holidays. Her daughter Anuska had informed her mother, and Anumita made this plan to surprise her. Anumita's luck favoured this time because coincidentally, Shreya's wedding date was fixed just three days before that. Anumita was very happy and excited too and didn't realize that a car was following her car.

Anumita's hotel was close to Netaji Subhash Park, and last time both visited Willingdon and Bolgatty islands by availing local ferries through waterways. Ernakulam is one of the busiest business centres and Kerala's most popular tourist spot. Anumita loved this metropolis because of the fascinating mixture of the old and the new. Ernakulam districts have many attractive places like Kochi or Cochin, one of the world's finest natural harbours. The Queen of the Arabian Sea, Kochi, was once a major centre for commerce and trade. The British, Arabs, Chinese, Portuguese, Dutch, and others came to its shores searching for exotic spices and sandalwood. Their traditional customary warmth and hospitality welcomed the visitors even now.

Anumita had reached the school and hurriedly entered with excitement. She didn't realize a man in the car was watching her from a distant closed window.

Anumita went to the Principal's office and waited outside as another guardian was talking with the Principal. Without her permission, she wouldn't be allowed inside the hostel premises. After waiting a few minutes, Anumita's turn had come.

"May I come in?" Anumita asked.

"Sure," Sister replied with a pleasant smile.

"Good afternoon, Sister," Anumita said.

"Good afternoon, please be seated," Sister replied.

Anumita took her seat and sought permission to take her daughter and Pritha for a short trip to Munnar and ensured that she could drop them back on Sunday afternoon.

"Yes, I got the mail from Mr Viswanathan, and he talked over the phone with me about allowing Pritha with you. I have no objection, but you should be very careful about both my students," Sister replied and called another sister over the phone.

Anumita had completed the official decorum and went to the hostel premises with a permission letter. After thoroughly checking the letter, the hostel warden informed them to come and meet in the visitor's room. Anuska and Pritha met her within a few minutes, and Anumita told them about the surprise trip she had planned. Both hugged her and shouted with joy. Anumita had told them not to waste time and come back within ten minutes with their luggage. Both ran away and returned after fifteen minutes. Anumita had noticed their faces and was so happy. Both had already started their plan for the trip. Anumita had entered the principal's room along with them to say thanks. Sister told her students to enjoy Munnar and take care of each other. Anumita assured Sister she would drop them off within the scheduled time and take care of them.

Anumita, Pritha and Anuska had come out and found their driver talking with the other driver. Anumita called him to place the luggage in the car. The driver came hurriedly, placed the bags, and started the car.

Anuska and Pritha looked so happy and were planning so many things. Anumita was extremely glad to see their happiness and remembered her school days with Shanta. They had travelled together to many places in India, conducted by their School as educational excursions every year. She had many sweet memories and always missed those golden days. Suddenly, it struck Anumita that she should call Mr Viswanathan and update him. He called Viswanathan but couldn't get the connection.

They had reached the hotel, and even this time she couldn't realise that the same car had followed her. All of them went to the room and freshened up. Anumita ordered coffee and some crispy and crunchy fries for everyone.

"Aunty, you gave us a big and pleasant surprise; we both never expected it. By the way, what about my daddy, had you informed him?" Pritha asked in a joyous mood.

"Just a minute," Anumita replied and tried his number again and the line connected.

"Hello, Mr Viswanathan, talk with your daughter," Anumita said and gave the phone to Pritha.

"Daddy, so happy, and thank you for this pleasant surprise, love both of you. Talk a bit with Anuska," Pritha said and gave the phone to Anuska.

"Thank you, Uncle, but we would have been more pleased if you could join us, if possible, please come, we all will enjoy it together," Anuska said.

"Thanks for your invitation. You enjoy it as much as possible and take care. Don't hesitate to call me at any time if you need me; I have some connections there who will help you with any sort of problem," Viswanathan replied.

Anuska had given the phone to Pritha, and after talking with her father for a few minutes, she hung up.

Anumita told Pritha and Anuska to get ready for an evening walk and buy some essential things. Within five minutes, they left the hotel and walked to Marine drive, another beautiful place in Ernakulam. The famous backwater and Cochin harbour can be seen from here, and the site is packed with shopping malls, cinema halls, high-risers and Cafe shops. The rainbow bridge on Marine Drive has another attraction for tourists. Anumita had visited this place several times, and each time she enjoyed it, a lovely stretched pavement for walking. Most of the elderly people walked here during the morning and evening. After half an hour of walking on Marine Drive, they went to the nearest shopping mall. Anumita quickly bought some essential commodities and confectioneries for the trip and returned to the hotel.

She talked to the manager and was informed that the same car and driver would be waiting for them tomorrow at seven am. They all went to the dining hall and ordered dinner. Some people were busy eating and a few waiting for their orders. Anumita noticed a person in Arabian dress reading the newspaper. His face resembled someone else's, but Anumita couldn't think of who. Suddenly, she found the person was looking at her, and she turned her eyes to Anusha and Pritha. They were busy with their planning for the next three days. Waiting for food was always cumbersome for her from her childhood. Even in the hostel, she was scolded by Shanta many times. Anumita was foody from her childhood and preferred varieties of preparations. But, after the disappearance of Hardik, she was so depressed that she had some chronic gastric problems and loss of appetite.

The waiter served their soup, and it was delicious. Both girls were enjoying that, and meanwhile, they ordered the main course. Suddenly, Anumita found that the person with the Arabian dress was not there. Anumita thought, he must have finished his dinner and had left She had started talking with Pritha about which subject she liked and came to know that she loved Mathematics and in future, she wanted to be a Mathematician, though her daddy's choice was Computer Science. She asked Anuska about her preference though she was well aware of her choice, still hoping that her mind might have changed. Anuska, as usual, answered that she wanted to be a nurse and devote her life to the needy.

Anumita and Pritha appreciated it a lot. They were all enjoying their food when suddenly a man entered the dining hall and took a seat beside them. The man was wearing a turban. He was a bit loud with the waiter and asked about the Punjabi food. Anumita realised the accent of the man was not like a Punjabi guy. Anumita looked at the face and again found some similarities, but she didn't express anything to the girls. They had finished dinner and went to their room. Anumita had made a call to Shanta and informed her of everything. Shanta was thrilled to know about the Munnar trip with her daughter and friend. Shanta had told Anumita to call her every day while staying at Munnar and take care of what she ate. After finishing the call, all of them went to bed. Girls slept off within a few minutes as they had a hectic schedule in school and had walked a lot in the evening, but Anumita couldn't sleep. She was trying to remember those two fellows she had seen in the dining hall, both were well-known faces, but right now she couldn't recognize them.

She didn't know when she slept off, awakened after hearing the soft knocking sound of the door. She initially thought it might be her mistake. Anumita was waiting for that knocking sound but couldn't hear anything. She found both girls were in deep sleep. Anumita was trying to sleep but couldn't. She got up and went to the washroom. Suddenly, she heard a slow crying sound from the adjacent area and attempted to recognize the source. She realised that the sound was coming from the adjoining bathroom. Anumita was scared and went to bed. She could not sleep at all. She again went to the bathroom and tried to listen to that sound but couldn't trace it.

She came back to bed, and it was around three am. Suddenly, she heard something pass through the corridor. Anumita very carefully stood near the door and tried to identify the sound. She realized something heavy was being dragged through the corridor. Anumita was scared to open the door but felt that something suspicious was going on in the next room. She went back to bed and tried to calm her mind and get some sleep but that didn't happen. Anumita had stayed at this hotel several times before in the last five years and had never faced such a situation before. She was confused about whether she should inform the manager in the morning or not.

Her daughter's call awakened Anumita. She found both girls were ready and watching her. She immediately left the bed and went to the bathroom. Within fifteen minutes, she got ready and left the room. Anumita noted that the sweeper was washing the corridor, she alerted both girls to walk carefully, and ultimately, they reached the reception. Anumita found the driver was waiting near the car and talked with that Punjabi guy, whom she had seen in the dining hall during last night's dinner.

Anumita didn't say anything to the manager, paid the bills and called the Driver to keep the luggage in the car. She came to know that they would be reaching Munnar within six hours.

After starting from the hotel, Anumita was relieved. She couldn't share anything with anyone and was stressed. She was confident that something had happened in the hotel yesterday night as she listened to the weeping sound followed by something being dragged through the corridor. Both girls enjoyed the journey and talked a lot, and Anumita felt relaxed. Anumita requested Bilal, the driver, to stop the car at a suitable restaurant for breakfast. After another fifteen minutes of the drive, Bilal told her that soon they would reach a waterfall, and there was a fine restaurant nearby. They could enjoy their breakfast along with the magnificent view of the waterfall.

"Oh! that would be fantastic," Anumita replied with excitement.

Anushka and Pritha were enjoying biscuits; their eyes fixed at the scenery outside the car. They talked about the Western Ghat Ranges, which they had learnt in standard seven Geography books. The Nilgiris hills are considered a famous range of Western Ghats, widely spread throughout India - Tamil Nādu, Karnataka and Kerala.

"Aunty, why is it called Nilgiris or Blue mountains?" Pritha asked.

"The reflection of the sky's blue colour throughout the ranges made the appearance blue, that might be the reason, though not sure. According to some other beliefs, the name blue mountains may be because of a flower, Neelakurinji, which makes the entire range appear blue," Anumita replied.

"Madam, you are right," Bilal replied.

"Wow, that's great. Bilal Uncle, can we see Nilgiris from Munnar? Anushka asked.

"Definitely, from Eravikulam National Park, you can see it, only twelve kilometres from Munnar bus stand," Bilal replied.

"That's great; will we go there, Aunty?" Pritha asked.

"Why not? Sure, we will make a trip for that, Pritha," Anumita replied with a beautiful smile.

"Keep quiet, listen to those sounds, they are gradually increasing," Anushka curiously said.

"Yes, Anu, you are right," Pritha said.

Anumita was a little nervous and was trying to find out the sound source. Bilal told them they were approaching the waterfall, so the sounds. Pritha and Anuska attempted to locate the waterfall from the window but couldn't find it. Bilal told them they could only see from the opposite side. After one minute, driver Bilal stopped the car and parked it near the restaurant. Girls jumped out of the vehicle and ran towards where they could see the waterfall. Anumita started laughing to observe them and didn't say anything. She understood their feelings because she spent many years in the hostel during school days. Sometimes, it was horrible and suffocating too. She allowed them to enjoy themselves independently, at least for these three days.

Anumita got down from the car and proceeded towards the waterfall. She noticed that both girls were observing it from a viewpoint. Anumita went there and shot their pictures, both were very excited. Suddenly, Anumita found the same Punjabi guy busy clicking a few snapshots of the Waterfall. Anumita thought this guy must be a tourist.

"Uncle, can you take one picture of us three in our camera please," Anushka asked that Punjabi person and realized he was the same person from yesterday's dining hall.

"Sure, give me your camera, and take your preferable position," The Punjabi guy said.

The guy took a few shots for them and went to the restaurant for breakfast. After spending five minutes, Anumita and the two girls went to the restaurant for breakfast as well. She couldn't find the Punjabi guy there.

Bilal had his breakfast earlier and was waiting in the car for them.

After eating Anumita, along with the girls, were seated in the car, and the journey resumed.

"Bilal, how much time would it take from here to Munnar?" Anumita asked.

"Two hours Madam," Bilal replied.

"That's fine; within one p.m., we will be in our hotel," Anumita said.

"Mummy, what would be the evening programme?" Anushka asked.

"Complete rest, darling, tomorrow we will have a trip the entire day," Anumita replied with a smile.

Anumita realized that both girls were disappointed with the plan, but they didn't argue. Anumita felt sleepy but tried to stay awake, as sitting beside the driver and sleeping is never wise. Anumita had noticed Anushka and Pritha both enjoyed the beautiful hills full of tea plantations.

"Madam, within half an hour, we will reach Munnar," Bilal replied with satisfaction.

"Bilal, probably I had mentioned to you about our hotel," Anumita said.

"Yes, you had told me about Hotel Paradise," Bilal replied.

"That's good. Is it far from the central city? Anumita asked.

"Yes, Madam, it's five km away from the main place, not very far, one of the best Hotels of Munnar," Bilal replied.

"Wow! That would be fantastic," Anushka said with excitement.

Suddenly, Anumita saw a beautiful resort from the window, and it was very close to their car. It looked like a fort above the hill.

"Bilal, I think we are very close to our hotel, and I guess that is the one," Anumita said after showing him.

"Absolutely Madam, after this turn, the entry gate would come," Bilal replied.

Anumita and the girls were busy observing the beautiful views and ultimately reached their hotel.

After reaching the hotel reception, the hotel staff welcomed them with their rituals and allotted them a nice room. Anushka and Pritha were thrilled and enjoyed the natural beauty from the balcony. Anumita was very happy to see them so joyous. She made a phone call to Viswanathan and told him about everything. Viswanathan told her if she needed any sort of help, she could contact the Manager without any hesitation.

"Hello, uncle," Anushka shouted from the balcony.

"Hi, what a surprise! again, we are in the same hotel," the man said.

Anumita went to the balcony after listening to their conversation and found Anushka talking with that Punjabi guy. The guy was standing on his balcony, just next to their balcony and watching the beauties of nature. Anumita and the guy exchanged formal smiles, and she went back to the room. Anumita was scared as that Punjabi guy from yesterday, and the other man's face resembled someone she couldn't remember correctly. She ordered lunch and went to the bathroom.

CHAPTER 6

THE SURPRISE

Viswanathan was thrilled to talk with Anumita over the phone and had decided to give them a great surprise. He informed his office staff about the urgency to go to Munnar, returned to his home, packed his luggage, and got on a bus.

After a long time, Viswanathan travelled by bus and was very excited. He liked the bus, sleeping and seating arrangements there. He booked a sleeping seat, and it was well arranged. It was the first experience of Viswanathan enjoying a sleeping seat during the bus journey. The conductor told him that they would reach Munnar within six am. Viswanathan was thrilled to see their reaction on seeing him in Munnar.

Viswanathan was awakened by the bus's sudden halt and noticed that passengers were getting off the bus. He realized that the bus had stopped in a popular food hub for dinner. At least six buses were parked there.

He got off the bus and had his dinner. The quality of the food was not bad. The thing he liked the most was the well-mannered staff. Viswanathan came back to his seat and looked outside through the window. He realized that many couples were going to Munnar, and some might be newly married, the golden days of life.

Viswanathan was nostalgic and remembered those days. They had their honeymoon in Kashmir for a week. Most of the time they spent in the hotel room. It was an arranged marriage fixed by both families, and his wife was so pretty that people could not stop talking about it.

Viswanathan, at that time, looked very handsome and masculine. Initially, he felt good when some of his close friends and relatives praised her beauty but gradually became irritated with this topic. Viswanathan had realised that he had become jealous of her. Whenever they went outside, most people looked at her, and sometimes their gestures toward his wife were so irritating and disgusting for him, but he never reacted to them but rather avoided them.

Viswanathan realised that his wife enjoyed his jealousy and always laughed at him. He got more irritated but didn't express it. One day both had a hot talk, and she blamed him for his attitude. Later, she told Viswanathan that if people were attracted to her, she how could she stop them. She didn't like to provoke anyone; men have this type of attitude by their nature. That didn't mean she intentionally encouraged them. Both had felt that a distance gradually developed between them.

After the birth of Pritha, she resigned from her job and entirely concentrated on looking after her daughter. Viswanathan never expected she would leave him so early. After losing her, he was so depressed that he started neglecting their only daughter. Pritha was only seven years old and was in standard three at that time. One of his close relatives had suggested admitting her to a residential School.

Initially, Viswanathan didn't like her as she was very close to her mother and avoided her father. Pritha was just a replica of Sujata, and Viswanathan was worried about her beauty. He had decided to admit her to the Residential School in standard four.

After her admission, Viswanathan was free and happy. Many of his relatives and close friends suggested he marry someone, but he restricted himself. Sometimes, bodily demands were extreme, which hurt him significantly, even though he didn't know how he denied himself. After admitting her to the Residential School, Viswanathan felt absolute loneliness, which was the turning point in his mindset. Gradually, his affection and responsibilities increased for Pritha. He missed both his wife and daughter all the time.

Viswanathan realised that he had searched for Sujata within her daughter after she left, but when both disappeared from his daily life, he felt the actual pain for Sujata. Most of us don't value something when it is with us. The first year was horrible for him; when Pritha was admitted to the School, he went to Cochin every month to meet Pritha, and this practice gradually became less frequent. Pritha demanded to go back home in every meeting, but somehow Viswanathan managed her and felt more affection. Pritha was reserved and matured from the early days. She looked like her mother but had a personality like him. After staying over in this Convent School, she became more mature. After the friendship with Anushka, she stopped asking to return to her home. Thinking of all these things, he didn't realise when he slept off.

Viswanathan awakened when the bus reached Munnar. The daylight had just appeared. He opened the bag and wore a jacket. Many passengers were still sleeping and the conductor loudly announced to evacuate the bus.

Viswanathan got down from the bus and booked an auto-rickshaw for the hotel and within fifteen minutes had reached the hotel. He was very excited imagining their reaction. Viswanathan waited at the reception, and the receptionist called the manager over the phone. Within fifteen minutes, his friend came and took him to his room. Viswanathan freshened up, and Rudra made tea.

They met after a long time, though they connected over the phone. Rudra always introduced himself as the hotel manager; only a few close people knew he was the hotel's proprietor. Rudra, being a bachelor, led his life on his own and was happy with his status. Viswanathan liked him, always inspired by his self-dependent attitude and hardworking abilities. He was the only college friend he invited and was present at the wedding ceremony. Rudra often asked them to visit Munnar, but somehow it wasn't possible.

They had a long conversation, two friends catching up after a long time. Both were immensely happy and had decided to spend some good times in Munnar for two days. Rudra opened the other room and told him to stay with him for two nights, and Viswanathan gladly accepted it. Viswanathan told him that his daughter still didn't know that he was there. Rudra told him the right time to surprise her and called a boy to take him to their room.

Anumita opened the door and was speechless.

"What a surprise! You at last came; I can't believe it," Anumita said.

"That's unexpected; where is Pritha?" Viswanathan said with a smile.

"She is in the bathroom; please come in," Anumita replied.

Anushka was on the balcony, talking with that Punjabi Guy, whom she couldn't recognize, Pritha's daddy came into their room. Anumita called her; she immediately went to the room and shouted with joy. She went to the washroom and shouted, "how long will you be there? Have you finished your bath?

"Yes, will be out in one minute," Pritha replied from the inside.

Anushka held her Uncle's hand and pulled him into the balcony. Pritha came out of the washroom and found both laughing at her.

"What happened? Am I late?" Pritha asked looking at both.

"No, dear, it's your friend who disturbed you," Anumita replied with a naughty smile.

Anushka ran away to the balcony as she knew that Pritha could pinch her. Pritha followed her and found Anushka hiding behind her daddy. She was speechless for a while and hugged her daddy. Viswanathan started laughing and was happy to see her daughter's joyous expression. Anumita came to the balcony, and Pritha hugged her with joy. Both parents were a bit emotional when they felt their happiness.

The Punjabi guy observed everything from his balcony and entered his room. He tactfully found out of the day's plans from Anushka but was disappointed by the sudden presence. He tried to understand the relationship between them. There was no doubt Anushka was the daughter of that lady, and the second girl would be this man's daughter. Were both in a relationship? He realized that in the presence of this man, his purpose might not be easy. He went to the dining hall and engaged in breakfast. After a few minutes, Anumita, Anushka, Pritha and Viswanathan entered and had started their breakfast.

After finishing the breakfast, they all went to the reception, and Viswanathan introduced his friend Rudra as his college friend and manager of the hotel.

"Where do you want to go first?" Rudra asked Anumita.

"You, please suggest we have our hired car," Anumita replied with a smile.

"Okay, call your driver. I will guide him," Rudra replied.

Anumita called him over the phone, and Bilal came within a minute. Rudra gave him a piece of printed paper and told him to follow that. All the important tourist spots of Munnar are mentioned there with distance. Rudra instructed Bilal to maintain the sequence of the sites so that they could easily cover the places.

Bilal assured him and went to bring the car. Anumita suddenly noticed that the Punjabi guy had started his car. Within a minute, Bilal parked the vehicle near the reception; they all got into the car without wasting time. Both girls were very excited and full of enthusiasm. Both parents were satisfied looking at their bright faces.

"Bilal, which is the first spot?" Anumita asked.

"Eravikulam National Park," Bilal replied.

"How far is it, and what will we do there?" Pritha asked.

"It is about fifteen kilometres from here and famous for certain flora and fauna: the Nilgiris ranges, one of the most spectacular spots of Munnar. We have to take permission from the forest department for entry and but no one is permitted to enter the core zone," Bilal replied.

Girls were excited as they would be able to see the Nilgiris ranges. Anumita had found the hills were looking like green tortoises, she expressed her feelings, and all agreed. Most of the small and big hills were full of Tea plants, and most of the local people worked in Tea industries.

"I read somewhere that Eravikulam National Park is famous for the Nilgiris Tahr," Viswanathan said.

"Yes, Sir, you are right, and you could easily find them, even if they will come to you as very friendly and docile," Bilal replied.

"Oh! We will take photographs with Nilgiris Tahr," Anushka said with joy.

"Yes, love you, aunty, for this surprise trip," Pritha emotionally expressed herself.

Anumita hugged both of them and felt so happy. Viswanathan was smiling at them from the front seat.

"Do you know girls who are Nilgiris Tahr?" Viswanathan asked.

"Yes," both shouted at a time.

"They are a special type of goat and have become an endangered species," Anushka replied.

"Right," Viswanathan said with satisfaction.

"I forgot to mention; you could see the Anamudi peak from the southern side of the park, the highest peak of Nilgiris Mountain," Bilal told them.

"Wow! That's great, thanks, Mummy, it's a part of our education too," Anushka said with joy.

Both girls hugged her from the two sides. Viswanathan got emotional and was impressed, but he didn't express himself. The first time he felt a soft corner for a woman after the loss of his wife. He had tried to remove the thoughts and was busy enjoying nature.

The car stopped, and Bilal said, "Sir, you have to take permission and entry tickets from the counter."

"Okay, all of you wait here; I am coming within a few minutes," Viswanathan replied and went towards the counter.

Anumita and the girls got down from the car and looked at the surroundings. Anumita found only three cars waiting there and suddenly she noticed the Punjabi guy was coming toward in his car. Anushka and Pritha saw him and shouted Gurjeet Uncle.

"Oh! Are you also sightseeing? Nice to meet all of you again. Will meet you on the spot," Gurjeet replied and started his car.

Anumita was uncomfortable as this guy was all along with them from the Cochin hotel. Moreover, Anumita had a bad experience that night at the hotel, though she never discussed it with anyone.

Viswanathan came with permission and entry tickets, and all of them started for their destination.

"The entire park is divided into three zones, core, buffer and tourists. Tourists zone is another five kilometres from here, and further entry is not permitted for the tourists," Viswanathan said.

"Yes, Sir, but you will get to see everything from the tourist zones, the Nilgiris Tahr, Anamudi peak, Nilgiris hills and a portion of lakes," Bilal said to them.

"That's great," Viswanathan replied.

They reached within ten minutes and found a few tourists enjoying Nilgiris Tahr. Pritha and Anushka, getting down from the car, started running to touch the animal and both parents, along with Bilal started laughing. Viswanathan and Anumita started walking and relaxed, and Bilal was seated in the car.

"Thanks, Madam, for this beautiful idea. See how they are enjoying it?" Viswanathan said.

"Yes, that's true, and I am sure if my daughter came alone, she couldn't enjoy it so much. Both have an excellent understanding and deep feelings for each other," Anumita said.

"True, I have found many changes within her after intimacy with Anushka, she is happy and joyous. Before she met your daughter, she was just like a robot," Viswanathan said.

"Even I have noticed many changes within my daughter," Anumita said.

Both sat in a chair and enjoyed nature. Girls asked them to join, but Anumita told them to enjoy themselves. Anumita noticed that Mr Gurjeet was busy with photography. Anumita told Viswanathan everything that happened from Kochi. Viswanathan assured her of watching that guy and not bothering him much as sometimes coincidentally, things happen in our life. Anumita didn't respond, and both started walking toward their daughters.

Both were sitting in a place and observed nature without talking with each other. Anumita sat beside Pritha and tried to find out their motives but couldn't. Viswanathan was a few meters away and noticed them.

"What a serene place Aunty! The first time we both realised that nature and silence strongly affect our minds, feeling a positive power within," Pritha said.

"That's true, Pritha. When you both will reach our age, you would feel it more precisely," Anumita replied.

Viswanathan had left the place gradually, feeling immense pleasure from walking around alone. The distant mountains were looking bluish, and he could realize the justification of the name Nilgiris. It looked so beautiful as the sky was clear and there was bright sunlight.

After walking about half a kilometre, Viswanathan had found the Punjabi guy was sitting in a place and busy with his camera.

"Hello," Viswanathan said.

Gurjeet turned his head and smiled.

"Are you a professional photographer?" Viswanathan asked him.

"Yes, a freelancer, and you ?" Gurjeet replied.

"Working in a multinational company," Viswanathan replied.

"Okay, I will see you again as my photography session starts now," Gurjeet replied and started walking.

Viswanathan stopped there and found the person was going towards a slope of the mountain and disappeared within a minute. He went back and found

Anumita, and the girls were not there. He tried to find them and heard Pritha shout, "Daddy, we are here."

Viswanathan turned back and noticed they were sitting on the steps of the opposite mountain. He raised his hand with a pleasant smile.

They all went back to the car parking area, and Bilal started the car.

"Which one is our next destination, Bilal?" Anumita asked.

"Mattupetty dam," Bilal replied.

"How far from here?" Viswanathan asked.

"Sir, about seven kilometres, within half an hour, we will reach," Bilal replied.

Viswanathan noticed that both girls were too excited, enjoying the tea gardens and corkscrew roads. Viswanathan was astonished to see the similarities between Sujatha and Pritha and suddenly became upset. He was confused and didn't understand whether he wanted to forget her or hold on to her memories within him. Initially, to forget her memories, he admitted Pritha to the Residential School. Viswanathan realized after a few years that both Pritha's presence and absence were painful for him, the most critical situation of his life.

Anumita noticed that Viswanathan was unmindful and looked upset. She asked, "What happened? Are you alright, Mr Viswanathan?"

"Oh! Nothing much suddenly was lost in some thoughts and memories," Viswanathan replied with a pale smile.

"After reaching there, first we will have some coffee, and then we will start for the Dam visit," Anumita said.

"Same here; need some coffee," Viswanathan replied.

Pritha and Anushka talked with each other all about the beautiful landscape of the surroundings.

All had coffee in Mattupetty dam and then had started walking towards the central observatory place. They found many local people enjoying a picnic and realized it was a popular picnic spot. Suddenly, Anushka found there were boating facilities; Anumita felt her excitement and said, "Mr Viswanathan, let's take a boat ride,"

"Sorry, I can't, please, you three, enjoy that. Otherwise, I won't feel comfortable," Viswanathan replied.

"Okay, Pritha, do you have any problem?" Anumita asked.

"Yes, Aunty, same reason, we both have hydrophobia," Pritha sadly replied.

"If Pritha wouldn't be there, the question doesn't arise for a ride," Anushka said.

"Don't be silly; enjoy riding with Aunty; we will shoot that; then we will spend time together," Pritha said.

"That's a nice friendly attitude Anushka. As we have come together, we would enjoy everything jointly," Anumita said.

They enjoyed the place by walking together. The place was serene except for the picnic places. Anumita had visited Cochin, Munnar, and her general observation was that Kerala's people were gentle and sober compared to others.

They went back to the car parking and found Bilal talking with other drivers in his mother tongue. After seeing them, he came back and started the car and said, "Our next destination is Echo Point, seven kilometres from here and another beautiful place in Munnar."

CHAPTER 7

THE ECHO

Gurjeet reached the car parking zone and found Anushka's car was not there. He blamed himself for this. Without wasting a single moment, he had started driving.

The Echo Point was very popular among the tourists as one's loudly produced sound reverberated. In between the three ranges, Mudrapuzha, Nallathanni and Kundala, there was a lake called Kundala lake. One can enjoy boating on the lake.

Gurjeet reserved one boat and went for a ride. The surroundings were beautiful and green. The slopes of the mountains were so lovely that strolling and trekking were very enjoyable. The boatman said that it would be more attractive when Neelakurinji flowers bloomed. Gurjeet realized that the tourists liked this place because of its versatility. He noticed that people were shouting at the top of their voices and listening to the echo. Gurjeet enjoyed this a lot and decided he would try after completing this boat ride.

Bilal parked the car, and they got down from the vehicle. They had decided to go for lunch, and Bilal escorted them. The Restaurant was excellent, and the food was too good. All enjoyed their lunch and appreciated it a lot.

After having lunch, they proceeded toward the lake. Imitating the other tourists, Pritha and Anushka started shouting their names and repeatedly called their friends' and relatives' names. Anumita and Viswanathan began to laugh and encouraged them.

Suddenly, a sound reverberated the place, so clear and prominent. Everyone heard the name 'Hardik'. Anumita was speechless and embarrassed, searching for Hardik everywhere but not finding anyone. She noticed that most tourists were searching for the person who created such a clear echo. Pritha and Anushka repeatedly tried to get the same quality of sound within a few seconds but failed. Again the same sound reverberated, but the person could not be found. Anumita felt uneasy and noticed that nobody else was bothered except her.

"Mummy, please say my name loudly so that I can enjoy your echo," Anushka requested her mother.

"Daddy, you too, call me," Pritha said.

Both started laughing and whispered for a second.

"Okay, let me call first," Anumita said and shouted the name of Pritha. Viswanathan had done the same thing. Both started laughing after watching their facial expressions. Pritha and Anushka were so happy and hugged them. Suddenly, Pritha shouted "Mummy," and it reverberated beautifully all over the area. Anushka repeated the same by yelling, "Daddy."

Suddenly, the whole situation changed; they became speechless and looked at each other's faces. Anumita and Viswanathan were embarrassed. Anumita had found both the girls were looking at them with pain in their eyes. Viswanathan realized the situation was going out of hand and immediately dealt with the awkwardness by shouting the name of Sujata. The whole area reverberated with the name of Sujata. Suddenly, Pritha hugged her father and started crying like a child. The mood suddenly became melancholic.

Anushka noticed her mother was looking very uncomfortable. Suddenly, the same sound, "Hardik", reverberated, and Anumita suddenly lost her body balance but escaped from falling due to Anushka. Anushka got hold of her and prevented her fall. Pritha and her father helped her to get up and to sit. Anushka opened the water bottle and splashed some water on her face. Within a few seconds, she got back to her senses and asked, "What happened to me?"

"Nothing much, you felt nausea and discomfort, so we washed your face with water; please drink some water," Viswanathan said and offered her the bottle.

Anumita had some water and tried to understand the incident. She felt awkward and said, "I am fine now. Let's proceed to that area."

"Are you sure you will be able to walk further?" Viswanathan asked.

"Yes, I feel comfortable and fit now, "Anumita replied.

They all made a round of the entire area comfortably, and Anumita had found girls became calm and quiet, all the time looking at her face. Anumita could feel her senselessness for a few seconds, changed the moment, and decided to return to the hotel.

They had reached the hotel without seeing two little places. Rudra asked about the trip, and Viswanathan told him everything.

"How are you feeling, Madam?" Rudra asked.

"I am fine now. For a short span of time, I had a horrid discomfort but within a few minutes became recovered from it," Anumita replied.

"That's fine, no worries, girls, it often happens during travelling. Let's have coffee together," Rudra said and ordered that.

They all sat together in the garden. Rudra asked the girls about their best experiences. Pritha said she liked everything about the Eravikulam National Park, especially the Nilgiris ranges and Anamudi peak. The opinion of Anushka was different; she preferred the entire road journey due to the tea plantation on the hills. The beauty of the corkscrew roads along with those mountains was unforgettable for the rest of her lifetime, she stated. Viswanathan said he liked most the innocent and timid Nilgiris Thar and Nilgiris ranges. Anumita didn't express anything, but Anushka and Pritha repeatedly asked about her opinion. She said Echo Point except for the part when she felt ill. Everyone started laughing.

"Echo Point is the most popular place in Munnar. Tourists generally don't miss it," Rudra replied.

The hotel staff served them coffee.

"Tomorrow, you must visit three more places in Munnar," Rudra said while drinking the coffee.

"Which are those, Uncle?" Pritha asked.

"Devikulam, Mattupetty and Top Station," Rudra replied.

"Wow! That would be fantastic," Anushka exclaimed.

"Yes, but you need complete rest and sound sleep for that as it's almost a hundred kilometres journey altogether," Rudra said looking at Anumita.

Anumita had started laughing, and all enjoyed it. She assured everyone about her freshness and fitness. Suddenly, Anumita noticed Gurjeet's car enter and crossed them. After finishing the coffee, Anumita requested another room for them. Rudra told her Viswanathan would stay with him in his quarter as they had met after a long time. Viswanathan also expressed his choice as it was within the same campus.

"We will have dinner tomorrow in my quarter," Rudra said with pleasure.

Everyone agreed to that and, after wishing each other, proceeded towards their room. Rudra gave the key to his quarter and asked him to rest; he would be coming after fifteen minutes.

Anumita and the two girls entered their room. Anumita went to the bathroom, Pritha and Anushka went to the balcony, and uncle stood there.

"Good evening, Uncle, how was your trip?" Anushka asked.

"Good evening, it was good. How many places have you covered?" Gurjeet asked.

"Three, and you please? Pritha replied.

"Same here, I spent more time in Eravikulam National Park, and I loved it" Gurjeet replied.

"I loved it too, beautiful in every aspect," Pritha said.

"Tomorrow, you are staying here?" Gurjeet asked.

"Yes, the day after tomorrow will be back to Cochin," Anushka replied.

"Okay girls, see you again, bye," Gurjeet said.

Pritha and Anushka were trying to feel the beauty of the last light of the day. The mountains were mystic and gradually faded away. Some people were going back to their homes, talking to each other. The sounds of their talking were so clear that they could listen clearly.

"I think my two girls are enjoying the beauty of the darkness," Anumita said with a smile.

"Amazing, Aunty," Pritha said.

"I will be back from the toilet," Anushka said and left.

Anumita and Pritha stood and discussed their studies and some funny incidents that had happened last month. Both were laughing a lot. Anumita noticed that Pritha had an excellent oration capability, and her expression was so good that it captured everyone's attention when she spoke. Suddenly, she found one shadow on their adjacent balcony, but it was not Gurjeet's shadow as no turban appeared. Anumita didn't say anything to Pritha, and both entered the room.

Anushka came back into the room after getting fresh, and then Pritha went.

"Mummy, are you feeling good?" Anushka asked her.

"I am quite comfortable, don't be upset. It may happen anytime to anyone," Anumita replied.

"You need sound sleep today. Let Pritha come; we will go for dinner," Anushka said.

Anumita's phone rang, and the call was from her friend Shanta. She told her everything except her senselessness. Shanta asked her about the Girls' enjoyment and they fondly remembered some unforgettable memories they had during their excursions many years back. Anumita started laughing like a school girl, and Anushka was so happy to notice that. Suddenly, Anushka noticed her mother stopped laughing, and her face turned pale. She realized that might be due to some bad news from Shanta aunty and was anxious to know about that. Anumita realized that her daughter followed everything, and she changed the topic and tried to make her laugh. It was not so easy but somehow she managed.

They rushed to the dining hall and found Gurjeet uncle was busy with his food on a distant table. They didn't disturb him by showing any courtesy. Anumita also noticed that the man enjoyed his food, and he was alone. They were waiting for the food, and Anumita got a phone call.

"We are waiting in the dining hall for the food; we will go back after finishing the dinner and sleep as early as possible. I am quite comfortable now, don't worry. Pritha and Anushka are with me and taking care of me. Want to talk with Pritha?" Anumita said and gave the phone to Pritha.

"Daddy, we are fine, and Aunty is doing well. Had your dinner? Okay, finish your dinner and take rest; good night," Pritha replied and handed over the phone to Anushka.

"Okay, if there is a situation like that, definitely I will contact you; good night, uncle, take care," Anushka replied and returned the phone.

The staff served their food, and they started to eat immediately without wasting time.

Gurjeet finished his dinner and went back to his room without saying anything to them.

All of them noticed that Gurjeet had left the dining hall. They saw other tourists started coming for dinner, and within a few minutes, the dining hall was almost full. One big family group talked with each other about their food choice, and it was confusing for the staff, but they were well behaved and managed their order intelligently.

The dining hall became lively within a short while. Both girls enjoyed that, and their eyes moved from one corner to another. Anumita was so happy to observe their glittering faces. They were interacting with some other tourists. They exchanged their sightseeing views. The entire dining hall reverberated with different sounds, and Anumita noticed that all the dining staff enjoyed it. After saying good night to everyone loudly, Anumita, Anushka and Pritha left the dining hall.

Pritha and Anushka started a walking race to reach the room, and Anumita strolled by seeing the surroundings, and when she crossed Gurjeet's room, someone whispered by opening the door slightly, "Anu, I am Hardik, would like to talk with you."

Anumita was scared and somehow entered her room. Pritha and Anushka were on the balcony and talking with each other. Anumita immediately locked the door and sat on the sofa. She felt discomfort and was trying to overcome it. She felt parched, and her legs were heavy, unable to bring the water bottle from the table. She noticed both girls engaged so profoundly in their discussion that they hadn't realized her condition. Anumita decided to sit over there for a few minutes without informing them. Suddenly her phone rang, and somehow, she opened her bag and received the phone. She found both girls were coming toward her.

"Yes, we are in the room and within five minutes will go to bed. Everything is fine, nothing to worry about; good night Mr. Viswanathan," Anumita said and asked Anushka to bring the bottle.

Pritha was busy making the bed ready, Anushka checked the doors, and Anumita went to the washroom.

They all went to bed and slept off within a few minutes.

CHAPTER 8

THE HOPE

Rudra and Viswanathan had finished their drinks and dinner, engrossed in discussing their college memories.

"Let's go to bed; it is already ten pm," Rudra said.

"Yes, that will be wise as we have to get up early in the morning," Viswanathan replied.

"Within Seven-thirty, it will be fine to get up," Rudra said.

"Really? Then we will have more time to chat in bed," Viswanathan said, laughing.

"Exactly, having such a nice time after so long," Rudra replied, smiling.

Both shared the same bed comfortably. Both remembered hostel days recapitulated some naughty incidents and laughed like young guys. Those days were golden days of life.

Viswanathan asked, "Rudra, do you feel loneliness as you have no one of your own?"

"Sometimes, but I have learnt to deal with it," Rudra replied with a deep breath.

"How do you manage?" Viswanathan asked.

"By engaging myself in different social projects," Rudra replied.

"Don't you feel tremendous sexual urges sometimes? Viswanathan asked.

"Oh! Sure, and after the age of forty-five years, it started to increase," Rudra replied.

"Exactly, sometimes it's irresistible, isn't it? I don't know how long I will be able to suppress it," Viswanathan said.

"Is suppression necessary? Why don't you marry again?" Rudra asked.

"Okay, I will; within six months, you will get an invitation," Viswanathan replied with a smile.

"I am not joking with you; go ahead. If you want, I will talk with one of my distant relatives, a nice unmarried lady about forty-two years old, fair complexion and a School teacher in your city," Rudra seriously said.

"Oh, my goodness! Do you also have a marriage agency? First, you get married, then give me suggestions!" Viswanathan said.

"I am a confirmed bachelor, no way to marry," Rudra replied.

"I am widowed; the question doesn't arise," Viswanathan said.

"Widowers can remarry, but once you are a confirmed bachelor, it is not wise to marry as the person declared himself the status," Rudra said with laughter.

"This came to my mind after spending time with this lady, and I would never hide my feelings to you," Viswanathan said.

"Hey, are you serious? Which lady?" Rudra curiously asked.

"I am not sure about it, but for the last few days, I have felt attraction for Anumita, for the first time after the death of Sujata," Viswanathan said.

"You meant the mother of Anushka! What have you found in her?" Rudra asked.

"Affection for my daughter," Viswanathan replied.

"Do you know her present status? I mean whether she is divorced or widowed?" Rudra asked.

"Not very clear to me as she or my daughter never discussed it with me; neither did I ask them. But I have never seen her husband with her on any occasions of the School," Viswanathan replied.

"Suppose she is widowed or divorced and agrees to marry you. Would you accept her daughter as your own?" Rudra asked.

"I will gladly do so as my daughter and Anumita have a beautiful relationship, just like two sisters, and you know very well that I can do anything for my daughter," Viswanathan said.

"If so, I will be happy too; the girls will have the love of both parents. But I guessed she is a working lady and not from your city; I don't know how you would manage that," Rudra said.

"She is a Scientist in the Central Government Organization. She also understands the tight bonding between the two girls. After her retirement, she could stay with me," Viswanathan said.

"Yes, that could be possible. You should definitely try that," Rudra replied.

"Now tell me honestly why you have decided not to marry.," Viswanathan asked.

"Because I have some biological problems and have suffered from Cryptorchidism from my childhood," Rudra replied.

"What is the meaning of that bombastic word?" Viswanathan asked.

"I have improper testis and impotence. So I avoided getting married and gladly accepted the hard truth," Rudra replied.

"Oh! Is that so? You have never mentioned it to me before. Did you consult with doctors?" Viswanathan asked.

"Testis had not descended from the abdomen during birth and sperm production was hampered but other male manifestations were fine as the doctor said.

My parents tried in several ways, even surgery in my childhood, but it could not be fixed," Rudra replied.

"I am so sorry, dear; I do respect your decision now," Viswanathan replied.

"Never mind, dear, I have accepted the truth from my adulthood and never felt distressed for that. I accepted my impotence as a challenge and realized that besides producing offspring, there are many things to do in life, one just has to stay motivated and positive," Rudra confidently said.

"You are right; people generally waste time by thinking of what they don't have and get demotivated, it's a negative attitude. We should always be happy with what we have," Viswanathan said.

Suddenly Viswanathan realized that Rudra had started snoring. He laughed and stopped talking.

Gurjeet was loitering in his room and was trying to think of how to reach her. He expected that she would ring his doorbell late in the night. He frequently went near the door to get the sound. He also watched from the balcony, but the door was closed, and soft lights came through the windows' glasses. Gurjeet was awake until late night but didn't hear any knocking sounds. He was upset and couldn't find a way to meet her. He had decided, that tomorrow he had to meet her by any means.

Anumita woke and found it was four-thirty am. She tried to remember last night's incident and thought to herself if Hardik and Gurjeet were the same people. Anumita found both girls sleeping deeply. She opened the balcony door very carefully and found no one was there, quite natural, the light of the room brightened the balcony. Anumita was confused and stood over there. She felt a peculiar sensation and her voice became choked. She tried to utter the name of Hardik but couldn't. She stood there for a few minutes and returned to her bed. Anumita realized her gastric pain had begun again; she had medicine and was relieved within ten minutes.

She suddenly recalled the information given by Shanta and was convinced that the person in the next room was none but Hardik. She had different questions on her mind. If he is Hardik, why was he disguised as a Punjabi guy? Why did he hide from others? Even in the second part of the wedding ceremony, he became quite comfortable in front of them. Why did he appear in disguise in Munnar? If he is not Gurjeet but Hardik, how did he enter the hotel without his Identity card? Anumita had decided she would clear it first thing in the morning. After confirmation of this man's real identity from Mr Rudra, she will arrange the next step. Anumita asked herself whether it would be wise to involve them in her most personal aspect of life. If the person was Hardik, it all of them would come to know there. She was confused, and her mind was not working correctly. This issue was such that even she couldn't take any suggestions from anyone, not even Shanta. Anumita knew that Shanta had somehow sensed she didn't want to share with her information about her marriage, husband and daughter. Even Shanta told her she was shocked when Anumita first informed her about her husband and daughter. Shanta initially expressed her grief, which was quite natural, but Anumita managed the relationship so nicely that it became like the previous one after four years. Shanta had promised never to ask about this issue until Anumita told her anything on her own. Anumita was cent per cent sure that Shanta considered it as a bizarre incident. But after that, both never raised this issue again, and gradually Shanta overcame the shock.

Anumita had never discussed anything with anyone except her parents. Of those who stayed at Jabalpur, only a few of them knew that. Most local people knew that their engagement had broken; the reason was unknown to most people. Hardik's college colleagues were astonished by the sudden disappearance of Hardik, and most of them couldn't find any reason for that as he was very reserved and never discussed anything about Anumita. They knew it when Anumita went to college and met a few of his colleagues after his disappearance. Anumita later realized that she shouldn't have been there to ask them about Hardik. But at that moment, she was so depressed and worried that she had lost her judgment and general thought processes.

She didn't make other mistakes when adopting Anushka. Anushka was only six months old when she adopted her. She had never hidden anything from her colleagues and relatives. When Anushka grew up and asked about her father, Anumita told her father left both and never contacted her again. Anushka was shocked and never asked a question about her father further to date. Anumita realized from her expression that she had tremendous loathing for her father.

Anumita asked her daughter several times whether she felt embarrassed when her friends or other people asked about her father. Anushka always told her she didn't want a father; she was happy with her mother and considered her more than two could be together. Anumita appreciated her thoughts and feelings, and never tried to marry another person. Sometimes it was difficult to control the sexual urges, but ultimately, she got over it. She realized that responsibilities were more important than individual demands and engaged herself for her parent's and daughter's happiness.

In the last five years, she lost her parents, and an absolute vacuum engulfed her within three years. Those days were another challenging period of her life, and she spent maximum time in the laboratory involving research activities. But there was always loneliness when she came back from her work. So, she had decided to return to Anushka after her board examinations. Her health was gradually deteriorating as her age increased.

Anumita got up, and it was six am. Girls were sleeping; she went to the bathroom; within fifteen minutes, she came and noticed the girls were still sleeping. She went to the balcony and found Gurjeet standing there and was speechless.

"Anu, I am Hardik. I am wearing a false turban so that no one can identify me, and you could maintain your privacy. I want to tell you the reason why suddenly I disappeared from your life. Please give me a chance, to tell the truth, probably the last opportunity for me and you too," Gurjeet appealed to her by carefully opening his turban and beard.

Anumita had noticed the person who stood on the next balcony was none but Hardik. She looked at Hardik for a few minutes; tears burst out from her eyes, her voice choked and became she couldn't move. Suddenly she heard Pritha call her; she went back to the room without saying a word to Hardik. When she left the balcony, Hardik uttered 'please'.

CHAPTER 9

THE CLIMAX

Rudra got up and went to the kitchen to make tea. He freshened up and asked if Viswanathan wanted tea. Viswanathan got up, immediately freshened up, and enjoyed the tea together.

"Shall I proceed with your proposal to Anumita Madam today?" Rudra asked with a smile.

"How will you proceed in this short time? It's better to wait for a few months and let me get to know her better. It may be my infatuation or some kind of sexual urge for long sex deprivation. Moreover, I do believe, Love should be mutual. Otherwise, it would be hell," Viswanathan answered.

"As you wish, but mind it, hit the rod when it is hot. Otherwise, it might not be there after thinking of so many pros and cons," Rudra replied.

"Let me know her physical condition today," Viswanathan replied and called her.

After talking with her, Viswanathan knew that they were almost ready, and within half an hour, they would be coming to the dining hall. Viswanathan learnt that she was physically fit, and both girls were very excited.

Anumita, Pritha and Anushka went to the dining hall and found a big gathering like the previous night. They noticed a few new faces there, but Hardik was not there. Anumita suddenly saw that Viswanathan was coming toward their table with a charming smile. He was looking fresh and attractive too. They wished each other and picked up breakfast according to their choice from the buffet.

"Where is your friend?" Anumita asked.

"In his chamber," Viswanathan replied.

"Is your friend married?" Anumita asked.

"No, he is a confirmed bachelor," Viswanathan replied with a smile.

"Okay, if he could spare some of his time, he could join us on this trip, we will be more than happy," Anumita said.

"True, you can invite him, and if he manages his duties with other staff, definitely he will happy to come with us," Viswanathan replied.

"Okay, let's ask him," Anumita replied.

They had enjoyed breakfast and went to the reception. Rudra was busy at the reception counter with two other staff members. A new couple and a small group of 6 members talked about their booking.

Viswanathan went there to speak with Rudra, but he came back after seeing that he was busy with the gathering.

"What happened, Mr Viswanathan?" Anumita asked.

"Rudra is busy with the newly arrived guests. I think it would not be possible for him to spare his time as it's the peak season for tourists. Let's go on our own like yesterday," Viswanathan said.

Anumita was a bit unmindful as her eyes moved here and there looking for Hardik. Both girls looked at Anumita, and Anushka said, "Mummy, uncle is saying something."

Anumita was embarrassed and said, "I am so sorry, yes, let's go like yesterday."

They all got up and went to the lawn. Anumita called Bilal over the phone, and the car reached reception within five minutes. They got up in the car and started their trip.

"Is everything alright, Bilal?" Anumita asked.

"Yes, Madam, Bilal replied with a smile.

"What is our first destination Bilal Uncle?"

"Devikulam, a nice hill station with a serene lake called Sita Devi Lake," Bilal replied.

"How far is it?" Viswanathan asked.

"Sir, it is around twenty-two kilometres from our hotel," Bilal replied.

The car left the town behind within fifteen minutes, and after that, everything around looked lush green. Small and big tea gardens passed one by one, and the altitude gradually increased. Viswanathan noticed Anumita looked at the window and had a silent, somewhat unmindful appearance.

"Are you feeling alright or any discomfort Mummy," Anushka asked.

"I am quite comfortable," Anumita replied.

"But you are looking exhausted and unmindful, Madam," Viswanathan said.

"Don't worry, I am fit and fine," Anumita replied with a smile.

Anumita tried to make herself fresh and stress-free by artificially smiling and talking with others but couldn't.

They reached the place after another forty-five minutes' drive—the entire area was covered with green hills, tea and rubber plantation almost everywhere.

They all got out of the car and found vast numbers of vehicles parked. Devikulam was another popular picnic spot and there was a boat riding facility at the lake. Because of its serenity, many people stayed here, on the outskirts instead of proper Munnar to avoid the crowds.

The lake was famous as it was believed that Sita Devi had bathed there, and due to the hot spring and mineral-rich water, it acted as a curative for different diseases.

The place was full of tourists, and Anumita found many picnic parties enjoying their way. Most of them came with their families and a big gathering near the boating booking counter. Anumita and Anushka loved boating, but this time they overlooked their liking as Viswanathan had some genuine problems.

"Uncle, where are you going," Anushka shouted.

Anumita suddenly turned and found Hardik laughing by seeing her daughter. He was in a turban and beard.

"Going for boating," Hardik replied and walked towards the ticket counter.

"Uncle, take care," Pritha shouted.

Gurjeet raised his hand without turning his head and vanished into the crowd.

"This man is suspicious," Viswanathan said to Anushka.

"Why do you say that? Any particular reason?" Anumita asked.

"This man entered the hotel as someone named Hardik. He had no turban in the picture on his Identity card, but then he started wearing a turban and the girls were calling him Gurjeet Uncle," Viswanathan replied in a low voice.

"How did you know that?" Anumita asked with astonishment.

"Yesterday, after coming from the trip, we checked the hotel register and found the details," Viswanathan replied.

"Why didn't Mr Rudra ask him?" Anumita asked.

"On which basis would he have asked him? A man can dress on his own without disturbing anyone. Don't worry; my friend informed the security guard to keep a watch over that person," Viswanathan said.

"Oh! But the person was innocent, very gentle and friendly with our daughters and not at all harmful," Anumita said.

"Maybe, but using this turban and his Identity card's picture shouldn't have been different if he has no intention, isn't it?" Viswanathan said.

"I think he came here either in an official investigation or any personal affairs and hiding so that people can't easily identify," Anumita said.

"Yes, but one thing is clear that he has no bad intentions at least with us till now. But my intuition is that he is following a specific person who stayed or travelled all along. Otherwise, we wouldn't find him to travel; he would be busy with that concern." Viswanathan replied and followed her facial expression.

Anumita was confused and replied, "Tomorrow morning, we will be leaving, so I have no concern about that, and you are now with us."

"But I am concerned as my daughter and you both are travelling together. I have decided to go with you up to Cochin and drop them at the hostel and you at the Airport. By the way, when is your flight tomorrow?" Viswanathan asked.

Anumita felt that Viswanathan had started suspecting her. She replied casually that her flight would be around six pm. After dropping them in the hostel, she will straightway go to the Airport.

"Okay, let me check whether I will be able to avail of any flight tickets around that time," Viswanathan replied by continually looking at her face.

"As you wish," Anumita replied as she understood Viswanathan was trying to reveal the relation between Hardik and Anumita.

"Can I ask you one question, Madam?' Viswanathan curiously asked.

Anumita was puzzled but managed somehow and replied with a smile, "you can ask any question except my personal affairs."

"Leave it; it was personal. If you have any questions, you can ask me," Viswanathan replied, smiling.

"Not as such, but one thing, why do you and Pritha have a fear of boating?" Anumita curiously asked.

Anumita noticed that Viswanathan's facial expressions immediately changed and became pale. Viswanathan replied that he had lost his wife in the Periyar lake boat accident. Pritha and Viswanathan survived somehow, aided by the rescuer. "We both have tremendous hydrophobia after that, now gradually regaining.

"I am so sorry, please forgive me," Anumita said apologetically.

"It's alright, Madam, now an old issue for me and habituated with this. Yes, loneliness is there but manageable," Viswanathan replied with a pale smile.

Anumita and Viswanathan observed both girls coming toward them. They were looking happy as they had complete freedom to move around. Anumita could understand their condition as she had spent maximum time in the hostel during her School and College days.

"Would you girls like to stay here for some more time or proceed to the next destination?" Anumita asked both the girls.

"Aunty, we loved this place and would like to spend more time here," Pritha said.

"Mummy, we will stay here for the rest of the time and there's no need to cover two other sites. From here, we will go back to our hotel," Anushka said with a demanding voice.

"Really? Do you both love this place so much? I have no objections. But tell me what you have found in this place?" Anumita asked with a curious smile.

"You tell first," Anushka said, touching the head of Pritha.

"This place and its ambience made my father so happy and relaxed that I had never seen before," Pritha said with pleasure.

All of them started laughing, and Anumita asked, "Mr Viswanathan, do you agree with her?"

Viswanathan was not prepared for this type of question, and he fumbled and ultimately swayed his head to yes.

"Wow, that's great, Uncle," Anushka shouted with joy.

"Now your chance Anushka," Pritha said.

"Well, my mother was pale and tense before reaching this place, and now she is looking quite comfortable and fresh. So, I loved this place because as far as both our parents are concerned, they are relaxed and happy," Anushka replied with a naughty smile.

Anumita and Viswanathan understood what they wanted to say and were embarrassed. Anumita tried to manage the situation and said, "something is wrong with these naughty girls, and I am sure it was pre-planned."

Anushka and Pritha started laughing, and Anumita said, "Okay, your proposal has been granted."

Both girls were delighted and started walking towards the lake.

"They are just like two sisters," Viswanathan said.

"Yes, Shanta and I were just like them. I enjoy their friendship and become nostalgic about my school days," Anumita replied.

"True, that's why I was worried when you mentioned that you wanted to take your daughter away from the hostel. After this trip, I am sure, it would be shocking for both; give them at least a few months," Viswanathan said with mental agony.

"My health is deteriorating day by day, and I realized that I couldn't combat the tension further. Jabalpur has many good non-residential Schools and would admit her to one of them," Anumita replied.

They went for lunch in a nearby restaurant and enjoyed the food. After having their lunch, they all went to the lakeside. Anumita suddenly found Hardik getting down from the boat. Both girls noticed that and started running towards him.

Anushka and Pritha asked about the views of the surroundings from the boat. Hardik explained them in detail with the recorded videos. According to their demand, he clicked a few pictures of them on their camera and found Anumita and Viswanathan sitting in a chair nearby. Hardik left the place without further talking with the girls. Anumita didn't give any importance to Hardik, and Viswanathan observed both Anumita and that guy curiously.

CHAPTER 10

THE UNREVEALED FACT

They reached the hotel and sat on the lawn like the day before. Rudra joined them a few minutes later and asked about their trip.

"It was superb Uncle, we enjoyed a lot in Devikulam and skipped the two others," Anushka replied with joy.

"Oh! Didn't you visit Top Station? You have missed a picturesque site of Munnar. Anyway, Devikulam is also a beautiful hill station and a popular one as well," Rudra said.

"We will come again, Uncle, because we love everything about Munnar," Pritha said with joy.

"Always welcome. Ask your father, I told him several times to come here and spend a few days, but he was so serious and particular about his job that he could not make any time. I don't know what happened this time; he, at last, came here," Rudra replied with laughter and ordered coffee.

Anumita realised Rudra's intention and just showed her ignorance. She was thinking about Hardik and couldn't decide whether she would meet him at night to know what he wanted to say. Probably he will try to say why he left her when he had fixed everything. Immediately Anumita's mind asked her why after so many years? Why not before? What to do with his reasons? If he asks for forgiveness, would Anumita accept it at this stage? Many questions came into her mind, and she was unable to solve her problems.

Viswanathan noticed that Anumita was restless and looked pale. He tried to change the topic and asked, "We want to reach Cochin within one pm, and what time have you suggested to start from here? Viswanathan asked.

"Sharp, Seven-thirty am, you would have to spare one hour for breakfast and lunch," Rudra replied.

"Okay," Viswanathan replied.

"What happened, Madam? You look exhausted," Rudra said.

"Really? Might be due to the hectic day outside; I need some rest," Anumita said.

"Okay, you rest and come sharp at eight pm, come for dinner," Rudra said.

They were ready to move to their room, when suddenly a group entered the hotel premises after completing their trip; they were very restless and tensed. All stopped there and tried to understand their conversations. It was then that they realised that they were talking about a car accident. When they came close, Rudra asked, "anything wrong, friends?"

"Sir, a terrible accident happened an hour back about ten kilometres away on the way to Top station," a middle-aged person said.

"Oh! Was there any casualty?" Rudra asked.

"Sir, the car had fallen from the road to about a thousand feet below in the valley. Chances of survival is almost nil," the person replied.

"How many passengers were there in the car, do you have any idea? Viswanathan asked.

"Sir, some local people reported three and a few others told a single person who was driving the car. But there was no confusion that it was due to brake failure," another young man said.

"Oh! Did anyone inform rescuers or civil defences?" Rudra asked.

"Yes, two or three local car drivers informed them. When we had crossed the accident spot, it was full of people, and everyone tried to locate the car," one of them replied.

Anumita stood like a statue, and another big group entered, discussing the same topic. It was clear that the rescuers had reached the spot and had started their operation. The next car's driver informed the rescuers that only one person was in the car and he was not from Kerala.

Anumita couldn't resist herself and asked, "was the person wearing a turban? I mean, was he a Sardar Ji?" Anumita's voice was trembling.

Anumita had noticed that Viswanathan and Rudra suspiciously looked at her; Anushka and Pritha were puzzled and speechless.

"Madam, that was not clear to anyone; a few were claiming that it was a single person and a few, more than one," one of them replied.

"Let's go to the room," Anushka said and pulled Pritha's hand.

"That will be better; go to the room and take a rest. I think within the morning, rescuers would solve the issue, and everything will be clear to us," Rudra said and proceeded towards the reception.

Anumita and the girls moved towards their room and Viswanathan towards Rudra's residence.

After entering the room, Anumita sat down on the sofa, and the girls opened the door of the balcony but couldn't find anyone on the next balcony. The door was closed, and there was no light reflection on Gurjeet Uncle's balcony. Both were speechless for a moment and came back to the room. Anumita looked at their faces and expected some positive response from them but couldn't get any. Anumita was not feeling good, and she went to the washroom. Anushka and Pritha sat on the sofa and talked with each other. Both were worried about Gurjeet Uncle.

Anumita came back after freshening up and was feeling better. Pritha and Anushka, one by one, freshened up. All had taken lying down on the bed and rested without much talking with each other. They felt some unexplained discomfort regarding this incident and somehow hoped that the victim was not Gurjeet, though there was no concrete evidence.

Anumita tried to control her emotions and tried to console herself by thinking that due to this person, her life had changed, and this selfish, cowardly fellow did not even bother to contact her, telling her the reason to leave her. After almost twenty years, when they met accidentally, that ungrateful person suddenly decided to tell the truth to her, disgusting. Anumita chose to harbour no more weakness and sympathy for that person. Suddenly Anumita's phone rang, and she picked up the call.

"Yes, we are fine, Shanta, tomorrow morning we will proceed to Cochin. After dropping them off at the hostel, I will go to the Airport for my flight. Is everything alright at your home?" Anumita asked and learnt that everything was fine there, and the newly married couple had reached Bali for their honeymoon. Pritha and Anushka enjoyed Anumita's conversation with her best friend, and gradually their moods improved, and both felt comfortable. Anumita also realized that the girls were enjoying their conversation. She continued her discussion, pleasantly remembering those days that they spent together in the hostel. Anumita intentionally talked about their funny experiences to make both the girls happy. Anumita realized that the breath-stopping situation was gone. Anumita cut the line after saying good night to Shanta.

The doorbell rang, and all of a sudden, their facial expressions changed. Pritha went to the door and asked, "may I know who is there, please?"

"Open the door Pritha, I am your Daddy," Viswanathan said.

Pritha opened the door, Viswanathan entered the room and said, "get ready, I am here to take you for dinner, let's go,"

"Give us five minutes," Anumita replied with a beautiful smile.

Viswanathan went to the balcony and observed that the next balcony's door was closed and dark. He saw that the person had not returned till then. The whole place was calm and quiet; moving lights were just looking like stars on the ground. After spending two days in Munnar, Viswanathan understood why it was called 'God's place.

They reached Rudra's residence instead of the reception. Viswanathan told them to avoid disturbance from the crowd of guests; they had changed the venue to Rudra's place.

Rudra welcomed them and offered them soft drinks. After a small discussion about Munnar's experiences, they started their dinner. It was terrific, and the girls enjoyed it a lot. The food was mouth-wateringly delicious. Rudra shared his different experiences of Munnar with them. Anumita asked about the proprietor and noticed that Viswanathan and Rudra were smiling and intelligently changed the topic. Anumita understood the issue and never repeated the matter.

After dinner, they strolled on the lawn for some time; Viswanathan and Rudra went up to their room and talked about what a great evening it was.

They entered the room, and Anumita locked the main and balcony doors. She requested both girls sleep as early as possible because they needed to wake up the next morning by five am. Anumita had taken one sleeping pill, and all slept off within half an hour.

Anumita got up and found it was four am. She went to the toilet, trying to remember what had happened last evening. She cautiously opened the balcony door and found Hardik standing there, without a turban and busy on his cell phone. She immediately turned back into the room with a pleasant feeling and thanked God for saving his life. She realized that Hardik had not seen her.

Anumita went to bed; she sensed an unexplained feeling of relief all over her body and mind. She realized that her love for Hardik, was still alive, it was not erased from her mind even at this stage of her life and after his betrayal.

Bilal started the car for Kochi. Anumita realized that it was better not to know certain truths when the due time has already passed in life; the past better be left in the past

Their car vanished into the blue mountains.